H.I.LL. FARM

MEGAN MOSIER

© Cover Design by Megan Mosier

Internal Artwork by Megan Mosier

Formatting by Loren Huxley

ISBN: 978-1-963140-00-2

✳ Created with Vellum

This book is for everyone who has ever encouraged me to keep writing.

You mean the world to me.

1: GRETCHEN

GRETCHEN HELD her ground as the Space Eel opened its great, toothy maw, eyes and spots flashing wild colors as it bore down on her. She aimed her plasma blaster in the direct middle of its throat and pulled the trigger.

Pew! Pew! Pew!

Sound effects matched the flickering lights that ran down the side of the gun, but it was no use. Lights flashed red and a neon sign beamed overhead.

GAME OVER.

"Ugh, this is the worst week," she muttered, removing her goggles as the hum of the game powering down thrummed around her. Smaller Eels—cardboard cutouts, wriggling out from a hole in a foam asteroid—came to a halt with a metallic squeal from the gears inside. The white, fluorescent lights blinked on.

Around the room, the buzz of conversation, mixed

with a few groans over the loss, became audible as other players grouped together. Gretchen tucked her curly hair back into her pink bandana, feeling out of place as she listened to them talk. Being a head taller than most, and the only one decked out in laser tag armor and a shirt from the prize table, she felt as if she stuck out like a sore thumb. She hung back as they made their way for the exit, but none of them noticed.

Gretchen shoved her blaster back into the charger at the doorway with a bit more force than necessary and stormed out of the room. "It's not like I care. I don't know them that well anyway."

Squinting as she entered the arcade, she paused and swayed while her vision adjusted. A cylindrical lava lamp on its pedestal by the laser tag room's door shed dim green light on the surrounding area. Gretchen trailed her fingers over the glass as she passed, feeling its warmth spread into her skin. It had been in the arcade for as long as she'd been playing, and she'd tapped it for luck every time she walked past it—not that it had ever helped. Its hum left a tingling sensation in her fingertips as she made her way to the cubbies.

The rest of the place was as thematic as the laser tag room and ten times as packed. It was Friday night, so no surprise. Fluorescent patterns adorned the walls and the sticky floor, and cutouts of glittery cardboard shooting stars hung from the ceiling. Other players filtered out around Gretchen, some of the younger ones heading for the brightly blinking games, while the rest, who looked to be a group of college-age students, headed for the exit. Gretchen's throat tightened as she watched them leave.

Peeling away her padded, lime-green armor, she plopped down on a bench beside the concessions counter. A thin, lanky young man in a Space Alien Laser Tag uniform side-eyed her from where he was working the popcorn machine.

"I take it the Eel ate you again," he said over the popping kernels and the beat of the electronic dance music.

"Shut up, Harley," she said, pulling her messenger bag from one of the cubbies behind her.

"Whoah! Someone's grouchy! Did this week's boyfriend ditch you at the last minute?"

"I said shut up," Gretchen mumbled, leaning back against the cubbies. His tone annoyed her, and she couldn't stop herself from adding, "I didn't invite anyone this time. I'm having a bad week."

Harley scooped a heaping load of popcorn into a paper bucket and carried it to a kid waiting at the register. When he didn't further acknowledge Gretchen, she cleared her throat and announced, "I got my exam scores back, and they were terrible."

Harley cocked an eyebrow at her as he began wiping down the counter. "Again?"

She sighed. "Again."

A screaming kid ran past the concession stand, causing them both to wince.

"You knew applying to vet school after taking so long a break from undergrad would be hard," said Harley.

Gretchen rubbed her ears. "But I didn't think it would be *this* hard!"

"Either you don't really want to do it, or you're not cut out for it."

Gretchen raised her head to give him a halfhearted scowl. She was glad the room was dark enough that he probably couldn't see the teary state of her eyes.

"What? I'm only telling it how it is. Look, Gretchen..." He paused to lean against the counter. "You've been coming here a year now, and I know you're not an idiot, but you expect everything to happen without any sort of pushback. You need to actually put the time and effort in if you want to change anything."

The words stung. Gretchen fiddled with the rim of her glasses and then pulled the messenger bag strap over her shoulder. She stood and took in the painted stars on the navy walls. They burned white hot beneath the blacklights and pulsed with the music.

"I'll be back after work tomorrow," she said, unable to muster the energy to make herself sound even the smallest bit happy. "I'm going to defeat that Eel someday."

She pushed through the front doors and stepped from the warm darkness of the arcade into the chilly March air. Though it was night, it was hard to see any stars from this deep in the city. The orange glow from the streetlamps tinted a few low-hanging clouds.

Gretchen rubbed her eyes, knocking her glasses askew as she made her way toward her car. "Harley doesn't know the first thing about me," she muttered. "He won't even hang out with me outside the stupid arcade."

But you really should've studied harder, said a voice at the back of her mind.

A buzzing noise snapped her out of her thoughts, and she drew her phone from one of the messenger bag's pockets and checked the caller ID. *Mom.* She grimaced. If she picked up, any hint of distress tinting her voice would elicit an avalanche of unwanted questions. If she didn't talk... well... same effect, just delayed. With a tight throat, she slipped the phone back in her bag.

Gretchen arrived at her car—an ancient, beat-up thing that somehow still carted her around reliably. She tugged on the door handle a few times before remembering to unlock it. Keys jangled together as she withdrew them from another pocket in the bag, and when she finally slid into the driver's seat and tossed the bag into the floorboard, she heaved a sigh.

One more try.

She could take the admissions exam one more time before the door to veterinary school was barred against her forever. Harley was right. She shouldn't have taken a break after she finished her first degree. But it was too late to do anything about it now. With a turn of the key, the engine purred to life.

The drive back to her apartment passed quietly. Exhaustion prevented any attempts to think up a better study schedule as the city streets rolled past, but by the time she reached home, her mood had somewhat lifted. She parked, cast a glance around the parking lot to make sure no murderers hid in the shadows, then pulled her bag over her shoulder and made a dash for her door.

Inside the apartment, Gretchen patted the wall until the palm of her hand found the light switch. *Click.* She frowned at the messy state of the entryway — shoes left where they'd been hastily kicked off, a haphazard stack of library books, an umbrella, still splayed open even though it had long-since dried. "I will clean this up tomorrow," she vowed, stepping out of her current pair of shoes. She dropped the messenger bag on the couch on her way to the kitchen.

A notepad sat on the table that occupied most of

the space in the kitchen. Gretchen reached for a pen and made a list:

Tomorrow
- Clean apartment
- Make a better study schedule!

She thought for a moment, then added:

- Beat Space Eel

Satisfied, she taped the list to the refrigerator and retreated to her bedroom to prepare for sleep. It was only when she returned to the kitchen for a glass of water that she heard her phone buzzing again.

"I better get this over with," she muttered. She snorted and then said in a high voice, "Gretchen, you should have studied harder! Gretchen, why don't you find a nice boy and settle down instead of going back to school! Gretchen, your dad and I worry about you!"

Composing herself, she pulled her phone out and answered it.

"Hey, Mom! I got my scores back and they were predictably atrocious!"

There was a small sigh.

"Mom?"

"Gretchen, sweetie, hi."

Something about the way she said it made Gretchen sit on the couch. "What's wrong?"

She heard her mother draw in a breath. "I'm sorry to be the bearer of bad news, but your great aunt Elsie passed away this evening."

Gretchen blinked. "I'm sorry to hear that. I didn't think you were close."

A pause.

"We weren't. But your grandmother is really upset, and she wants us to be there for her," she said. "I need you to come home tonight."

"Oh," said Gretchen, picking at a loose thread on the couch cushion. "But I have work tomorrow."

"Please take off. I need you. Your grandmother needs you," her mother said. "Elsie was so reclusive, there probably won't be many people there. We want to show our support."

"Okay," Gretchen conceded. She knew her great aunt had abandoned the rest of the family, but the thought of no one showing up to her funeral felt sad.

"We're leaving in the morning," her mother said.

"I can leave from here," Gretchen offered.

"No, I don't want you driving that death trap of yours out of the city."

"But—"

"Gretchen, please."

"Okay."

After hanging up, Gretchen flopped across the

couch and groaned. A funeral was the last thing she wanted to go to this week. She texted Harley: *You'll never believe how much worse my week got.*

Gradually, she relaxed. She supposed she shouldn't complain. Though the timing sucked, it would be horrible if nobody besides her grandmother showed up to mourn her great aunt. She checked her phone. No response from Harley. With a sigh, she set the device on the floor and lay down again. It was the right thing to do. And perhaps if no one showed up, it would be a short affair. Then, she could spend the rest of the day working out her new study schedule.

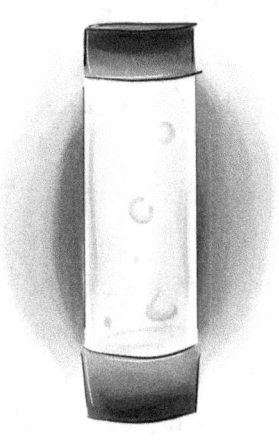

2: The Funeral

"This place is packed!" Gretchen's father exclaimed for the third or fourth time since they entered the parking lot. She'd lost count. They'd been circling it for ten minutes with no luck. Cars crammed almost door-to-door, filling every available space, and people milled about, heading in the general direction of the funeral home.

"We should park on the street. This is unbelievable," he muttered.

He swore under his breath and slammed on his brakes as a little girl darted in front of the car, causing the man in the truck behind them to lay on his horn. Even through the rain-spotted window, Gretchen could see mud caking the hem of the girl's puffy black dress, and that the pink-spotted umbrella, slung over her shoulder, was doing little to keep her hair dry. She wished her own attire was as fun. The plain black, sleeveless dress bunched uncomfortably as she adjusted her seat belt, and she shifted in her seat, hoping it wouldn't become noticeably rumpled.

"It's a good thing we carpooled," Gretchen's mother said, turning to smile at her daughter.

"No kidding. Great Aunt Elsie must've had a lot of friends," Gretchen noted as she watched the little girl catch up to her parents. She startled as her mother reached to tuck a stray curl away from her face.

"Did you register for your next test yet?"

Gretchen groaned internally. "I really don't want to think about it for at least a week."

Her mother frowned. "Sweetie, you have to think about it if you're going to do well." She continued to fuss over Gretchen's hair. "Is this really what you want? You know, you could always do something that doesn't require more school."

With a lump in her throat, Gretchen ignored the question and returned to people-watching. The girl and her umbrella had long-since disappeared from view, and now she could see an elderly woman in a sari talking with a man in thick spectacles. They paid no attention to the car as the Hollanders rolled past. She next saw a couple of tall men in cowboy hats climbing out of a truck. As hard as she tried, she didn't recall seeing either in any family photos. A group of somber-looking young adults who seemed to only be a few years older than herself stood nearby.

The glass of the car window felt cold against her nose. She couldn't find any sort of common thread among any of them, but it made something in her ache. As she and her parents left the parking lot and pulled onto the street, she took out her phone and texted Harley: *Would you come to my funeral if I died?* She watched the screen expectantly until her father parked in a tiny spot on the curb.

He probably wouldn't. He'd probably say something like *"She had it coming,"* and laugh. Perhaps her coworkers would attend out of pity. With a sigh, she returned the phone to her purse and clambered out of the car. The skirt of her dress twisted awkwardly, so she smoothed it as best she could and set out toward the funeral home.

GRETCHEN MET her grandmother beneath the awning in front of the entrance to the building. The older woman only came up to her chin, but her face shape bore a resemblance to Gretchen's own, and her hair, though much neater and shocked white with age, held the same waviness. She was dressed all in black, and even though she appeared composed, Gretchen could see small makeup smudges under her eyes.

"Grandma, I am so sorry," she said as she was pulled into a hug that crushed her ribs.

"Thank you for coming," her grandmother said.

She released her, stepped back, and looked Gretchen up and down. "Your mother says you failed your test again."

"Oh, um..."

Excuses sprang to the tip of her tongue, but she was saved from having to answer as her parents joined them.

"Hey, Mom, how are you holding up?" her mother said, stepping up to receive her own rib-crushing hug. Gretchen used the opportunity to slip through the doors of the building.

The sheer number of mourners in attendance overwhelmed her. Gretchen kept to the walls and edged toward a small, decorative column, awkwardly propping her elbow on it to steady herself as she watched. Not one person looked even vaguely familiar. She kept walking and observing and was surprised to catch snippets of conversations in various languages. *Did Elsie speak these languages as well?* she wondered.

"Are you looking for somebody in particular?"

A man appeared beside her. He seemed to be in his forties, and was shorter than her by a head. Like many of the men in attendance, he was dressed in a fancy suit and tie. Against the black fabric of his button-down, the metallic glint of a pin caught Gretchen's eye. Delicate metal formed the shape of a compass. Gretchen fixated on it as she answered. "No. Elsie was my great aunt. It's hard to believe she knew so many people. She must've been really nice."

The man adjusted his jacket, covering the pin. "Indeed. She was a kind woman. And smart. It was amazing to listen to her talk about her experiences. She will be sorely missed."

Gretchen turned away politely as he pulled out a handkerchief and wiped the corners of his eyes. "I take it you knew her pretty well?"

"I've known her since I was young. I would ask her over and over to tell me the story of when she climbed Mount Everest."

"Whoah, wait. My great aunt climbed Mount Everest? Did she reach the peak?"

The man nodded. "She said she trained for a year and a half. The ascent is extremely harsh—subzero temperatures and low oxygen levels— but when she talked about it, it seemed like all she remembered was the beauty of the mountain and the view from the roof of the world."

"That's amazing," said Gretchen. "Some days, I can barely climb the stairs to my chemistry class."

The man chuckled and they lapsed into awkward silence.

"Oh, uh, I don't think I caught your name," said Gretchen.

"Ah, yes. Introductions," said the man. "I'm Edgar Carsen. My wife and I knew Elsie well. We used to have dinner with her every Monday. She asked me to handle the funeral, and Penelope is handling her will."

Gretchen extended her hand and he shook it. "Nice to meet you, Edgar."

"And with whom do I have the pleasure of speaking?"

"I'm—"

A tall, red-headed woman in impressively high heels approached them, stress evident in the way her lips pulled tight. "Edgar! You're needed in the sanctuary. It's an emergency." She threw a glance at Gretchen and lowered her voice. "They're here."

Exhaustion fell over Edgar's face and he followed the woman without a word to Gretchen.

Gretchen stared after them, uncertain as to where to go, but she didn't have to worry for long. Soon, everyone began moving toward the sanctuary for the service, and she allowed herself to be swept along in the same direction. As she moved with the crowd, she tried to pick out her parents or her grandmother, or even an uncle—but it was almost impossible as the sea of people surged around her. In the end, she settled on a pew near the back of the room, and found herself wedged between a dignified-looking woman and a man who smelled like bubble gum.

The preacher approached the pulpit and a hush fell over the crowd. He arranged his notes, leaned into the microphone, and cleared his throat.

"We are gathered here today to honor the memory of Elsie Hildegard," he said in a smooth voice.

A small groaning sob caused Gretchen to turn in her seat. She had to do a double take to process the sight of the group of seven tall, hooded figures who had gathered behind her. One of the figures was bent in grief, trying to regain control of himself. The others stood close, heads bowed. Gretchen wanted to ask if they were monks, but refrained.

"Here," she said, taking a tissue from the back of one of the pews and offering it up to him.

"You are very kind," he choked out.

Then, to Gretchen's astonishment, he leaned forward, hood, brushing over her hand, and took the tissue with his mouth. Her eyes widened in confused horror, and she turned to face the front again before her freaked-out expression could betray her.

Throughout the rest of the service, the monks sniffed and murmured to each other. Gretchen rigidly faced forward, trying to tune them out.

DOZENS of framed black-and-white photographs decorated a long table against the wall of the foyer. They all depicted a tall, wavy-haired woman on various excursions— hiking through a rainforest, gently cradling a large starfish over a tidal pool, posing elegantly in front of the Grand Canyon. There was even a photo of the woman standing at the peak of what Gretchen assumed to be Mount Everest. The images contrasted her own vague memories of a frail woman she visited once in the early years of her childhood. It was hard to associate these memories with the stories she'd been hearing all day.

She glanced over her shoulder and caught sight of the monks, standing in a circle, hoods still drawn. They each leaned against a walker as they chatted. The one who had spoken to Gretchen still seemed to be crying, and for a moment, she felt the urge to comfort him. But the odd interaction from earlier gave her pause.

Reaching into her purse, she took out her phone and typed a message: What kind of monk picks things up with his teeth?

She stared at the screen, waiting for a response. "C'mon, Harley. I know you aren't working *that* hard."

After a couple of moments, she was rewarded with a *ding!* and opened the text.

HARLEY

I give up. What's the punchline?

GRETCHEN

Never mind. You're no help.

HARLEY

I'll give you a pass since you're grieving.

How was the service?

GRETCHEN

There's sooooooo many people here!

I don't know any of them!

My great aunt climbed Mount Everest!

HARLEY

Stop texting me and go be sad or something.

Grinning, she slipped the phone back into her purse. She returned to examining the photographs, but it wasn't long before she was pulled away.

"Gretchen!" came a hushed voice.

She stood and looked around.

"Gretchen, in here!" her mother beckoned from a doorway and then disappeared into the adjoining room.

Gretchen reluctantly pulled herself from the photographs. She smoothed a wrinkle in her dress and trailed her fingers through an arrangement of white roses as she passed into the room. It was bare of any decoration, and hardly provided the space for the twenty or so people who had been gathered inside. Gretchen didn't recognize any of them. She spotted her mother, dressed in a pretty black dress, standing at the edge of the throng.

"What's going on?" she whispered as she approached.

Her mother leaned in. "They've called all the great nieces and great nephews in here. I'm not sure why." She pressed a kiss to Gretchen's cheek. "I'm going to find my brothers and your father. Come let me know when you're done." She swept out of the room, leaving her daughter among the strangers.

Gretchen crossed her arms and shifted her weight between her feet as she took in the people around her.

The unfamiliarity was starting to unnerve her, and she was unsure how or if she should introduce herself. Besides, everyone was already engaged in conversation. She caught snatches of small talk as well as repetitions and analyses of stories that had been shared during the service. Apparently, she wasn't the only one surprised to learn of Elsie's many exploits.

A few people at the edge of the room clumped together, speaking in hushed tones. Gretchen couldn't make out anything being said, but from their expressions, it seemed intense.

They were interrupted by a sudden commotion at the back of the room. Edgar stood there, holding a box, and cleared his throat. "Hello! Yes, attention, please!" he called, bouncing on the balls of his feet. Once he was sure everyone was focused on him, he smiled warmly.

"Hello, and welcome. First, let me offer my

sincerest condolences." The corners of his lips twitched, and he cast his eyes downward and drew in a deep breath. When he looked up again, the smile had returned. "I had the pleasure of knowing Elsie for twenty years, and I will forever treasure her memory. The world has lost a great woman."

The crowd gathered before him, watching him with expectation.

"If you knew Elsie, you knew she loved to write letters. Before she passed, she made sure you would know how much she cared about each of you. So, without further ado, when I call your name, please come forward and receive your letter." He opened the box and fished out a paper envelope. "Alexander Arnolds!" he read off the back.

A tall, well-dressed man stepped forward and accepted the envelope, which was extended to him. He stared at it for a moment, muttered his thanks, then made to rejoin the crowd. However, a call from one of the guys he'd been standing near in the crowd stopped him.

"But you have to read it! Open it up!"

"Yeah, go on, Alex!" called another from the group. Possibly a brother, judging by his similar facial features. "We're all curious!"

"Alright, alright," Alex chuckled awkwardly. Inch by inch, he tore the flap up from the envelope. When the last bit of flap had been unstuck, he pulled out a folded sheet of paper.

"Dear Alex," he read. "I have always been so impressed by how smart you are. I was not surprised that you went on to be a doctor. I want you to continue to have a happy and purposeful life. Please accept this— Oops!" He fumbled with the letter and the envelope as another slip of paper fell out. He blushed and stooped to retrieve it. "Ah. It's a check," he said, still very pink as he read it. "That was very kind of her. I wish I remembered her better."

Gretchen stood on her tiptoes to see over the crowd as the next cousin, a woman with impeccable hair and makeup, got called to the front. She graciously accepted her envelope, and, like Alex, opened it then and there.

"Dear Whitney, you have grown into such a strong, confident young woman. I watch the news every day just to hear your reports. Save this gift, and I hope someday you'll be able to travel and find exciting stories wherever you go. It's a beautiful world out there. Lots of love, Your Great Aunt Elsie."

The trend continued as another cousin read her letter aloud—Elsie was so proud of her contributions to cancer research and offered a small sum for better lab equipment. Another cousin received praise for writing an award-winning book, and another for designing an efficient energy source. The prospect of an envelope addressed to Gretchen made her stomach churn. What could Great Aunt Elsie possibly have to say about her when they'd never actually met?

"Priscilla Snyder!"

A woman with a toddler balanced on her hip stepped forward. She had a frown that caused the rest of her features to pinch upward, as if she smelled something bad. The baby reached for the letter as she unfolded it. Unlike everyone else, she didn't read it aloud. Various, unreadable expressions crossed her face as her brown eyes scanned its contents. Finally, her eyes snapped back to meet Edgar's.

"This isn't what she promised me," she said.

"Oh, well... I'm sorry," he said awkwardly. "I have no idea what was written in these. I am merely the messenger."

The woman's frown deepened, and she looked like she might argue, but she said nothing as she returned to the crowd.

A few more names were called. Some read their letter aloud, but others only thanked Edgar and stepped back.

"Gretchen Hollander," Edgar said.

Gretchen suddenly felt rooted to the spot. She couldn't go up there in front of everyone!

"Gretchen?"

By now, people were craning their necks, scanning the room, despite not knowing what she looked like.

After a moment, she swallowed her nerves and approached the front of the room.

"Hi. I'm Gretchen."

Edgar's lips curved in a smile of recognition. "Very well." He reached into the box. Gretchen studied it. Carved designs decorated every available surface of the wood. She could make out flowers and mountains and llamas. He came up with her envelope and extended it to her. Gretchen stared at it, clasped in her hand.

She turned to face the crowd.

"I think I'd like to open mine later, if that's okay," she said, avoiding the stares of her cousins. No one protested, so she stepped back down and buried herself in the crowd.

A loud creak and a small *thump* signaled the lid of the box snapping shut. "Alright, folks. That is all," Edgar announced.

Everyone started talking at once. A woman's voice rose above the growing chatter.

"But what's happening with the farm?" It was the pinch-faced woman in the back.

"Excuse me?" said Edgar.

She shifted her toddler to her other hip. "Elsie's farm! All these notes are good and well, but who did she leave her land to?"

Hushed murmurs swept over the room again.

"I'm sorry, but as I said before, I am only the messenger. Now, I must attend the burial."

With that, he left. The chatter grew louder, and as Gretchen left the room, she noticed Priscilla approaching someone who had not read his letter aloud. She quickened her pace before she could be seen.

She set off, in search of her parents. She opened the door to a room and found Edgar speaking angrily and in a low voice to the seven hooded monks. She would've stayed to listen, had not her mother tapped her on the shoulder.

"Gretchen, we're leaving."

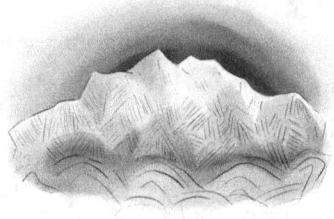

3: Elsie's Letter

"I'm back!" Gretchen called, pushing through the front door of the veterinary clinic. She'd been too tired to do laundry after her parents dropped her at her apartment the previous night, so she wore a faded, holey T-shirt and jeans. In one hand, she clutched the envelope from Elsie. The other gripped the strap of her messenger bag as she stepped into the warm waiting room, which smelled of bird poop and stale dog kibble.

"SQUAWK!" said a blue parrot on a perch by the door.

"SQUAWK!" said Gretchen, reaching out to let him nibble her fingers.

The room was otherwise empty. After giving the parrot a kiss on the beak, Gretchen made her way behind the receptionist counter and dropped off her bag and her jacket on the back of her rolling chair. Voices drifted from the break room, loud enough so that she didn't have to strain to hear what was being said.

"And apparently he left all the samples out of the refrigerator overnight!"

"Oh my! I can't imagine what was going through his head."

Ah yes, Gretchen thought, rolling her eyes. *That intern who got fired at the vet office on the other side of town.* Her coworkers had talked the subject to death over the last week, to the point where it made her uncomfortable to listen. The guy made a few mistakes. Gripping the back of her chair, she leaned back so she could see through to the back room and called over her shoulder, "Maybe he got distracted."

Her coworkers spared her a brief glance and kept talking. Gretchen waited, but they never looked back at her. She sighed and stashed her bag under the desk, then took a seat. The envelope weighed heavy in her hand, but fear of its contents overwhelmed her curiosity. It was much thicker than the others that had been given out. *Figures that it would take a whole novel to contain a stranger's disappointment in me.*

Shoving it in a drawer, she wiggled the mouse of the computer to wake it up and begin her receptionist duties. The screen sleepily blinked on, and she typed her log-in information. As she waited for everything to load, the phone rang.

"You've reached the Caring Paws Animal Hospital. This is Gretchen."

A high-pitched wail sounded through the phone's speaker. Gretchen pulled it back from her ear with a wince.

"Hello? What's wrong? Hello?" she said between the sobs.

She stood and paced as far as the cord would allow, waiting for the sniffles to die down. When they finally did, a woman's voice declared, "It's Mr. Pickles! He's sick!"

"That's no good! What's going with him?" Gretchen asked, careful to keep her tone light.

"The poor kitty won't come eat his breakfast. He *always* eats his breakfast!"

"Poor baby. Are there any other symptoms? Any wheezing or abnormalities with urine or feces?"

"He looks very sad," the woman said.

"I see," said Gretchen. "Can I schedule him a visit for tomorrow afternoon?"

"Yes, please!"

"And with whom am I speaking?"

"This is Lana Williams."

"Alright, Mrs. Williams! I have Mr. Pickles down for tomorrow at two o'clock!"

. . .

THE REST of the day flew by. Clients filtered in and out of the clinic, Gretchen answered phones and scheduled visits, and the rest of the staff tended to the patients. In the lulls, her mind strayed to the photograph of Elsie, standing at the top of Mount Everest. Everyone else's letters had been so nice, and the words held an undercurrent of pride—and they deserved it! They were scientists, engineers, linguists, artists, *explorers!* And Gretchen was...

"Gretchen!"

She glanced up to see one of the vet techs trying to get her attention.

"What's up?"

"Why did you schedule Mrs. Williams for tomorrow afternoon? We already have a surgery scheduled for tomorrow afternoon."

Her eyes widened. "No, I could've sworn..." She flipped through her calendar. There, on the block for the next afternoon, her own handwriting glared treacherously back at her: *Surgery for Spot the Dog!*

She groaned.

"My bad. I'm sorry."

The vet didn't acknowledge her apology. "Call Mrs. Williams and tell her to reschedule."

Gretchen picked up the phone again, her face pink with embarrassment. The dial tone sounded, but Mrs. Williams didn't answer, so she left a message. When she hung up the phone, her head sank until her cheek squished against the surface of the desk.

"Why?"

Her hands strayed toward the drawer with her letter. "Might as well get this over with. If the worst comes to worst, I guess I didn't know her anyway."

Paper crinkled as she procured the envelope. She ran it along the desk's edge to smooth it— a plain envelope, addressed to her in what she supposed to be her great aunt's curving handwriting. Turning it over, she tore at the corner until she could work her finger beneath the flap, then slid it to break the seal. Inside was a letter, written in the same neat script.

Dear Gretchen,

I haven't seen you since you were very small, but I have heard from my sister how you have grown, and I am very proud of you. I know how much you love animals, so I am leaving you my farm. Please look after my llamas. Especially Melville. I think the two of you will get along.

Much Love,
Your Great Aunt Elsie

Sharp pangs of guilt stabbed at Gretchen's stomach. She never would've been able to put a face to her great aunt's name before the funeral, yet she'd gone and left her farm to... to...

Gretchen balked as the meaning of the words hit her. "To me."

A farm.

Great Aunt Elsie left her a *farm*.

She opened the envelope again and found the source of its weight— a thick package of documents. She unfolded the packet and her eyes widened as they scanned the fancy fonts and dreadfully legal-looking format. The deed to the property. Gretchen rose to her feet, free hand moving with nervous energy to pull at her hair. "Oh no. No, no, no, no. What am I supposed to do with a farm?"

The Space Alien Laser Tag arcade was mostly empty at two o'clock in the afternoon. A few more lights were turned on than the other night, and the building was relatively quiet without the EDM blaring from the sound system. Gretchen pushed through the front door and made a beeline for the concessions counter.

"Back to lose again?" Harley said in greeting.

She slapped the envelope onto the counter. "I need your advice."

The situation came out in what felt to Gretchen

like a string of disjointed babbling. Harley pulled out the letter and the deed and looked over them with a creased brow. A kid approached the counter and demanded gummy snacks, but Harley only waved him away.

"Well? What do you think?" Gretchen asked after a few minutes.

"You can always sell it," he said.

"But she left it specifically to me," she protested. "Wouldn't that be disrespectful?"

Harley handed the papers back to her. "She's dead. She'd never know."

Gretchen took it, a dubious frown tugging at her lips. "You're not helpful or comforting."

"You said you hardly knew her!" he said with a defensive shrug. "My advice is to go check the place out, figure out how much it's worth, and sell it. You said so yourself—if you were in charge, it would fall apart. So technically, doing so would be the opposite of disrespectful. Poor little Melville."

"Hey!" Gretchen objected. "The llamas are the one thing I know I could take care of! It's the other stuff— the land and the house and the machinery. I wouldn't know where to start."

"Alright, then keep the llamas and sell the rest," Harley teased. "Look, there's a number in there for you to call. I would explain the situation. No one is forcing you to take it."

Gretchen took a deep breath and nodded. The noises of the blasters in the laser tag room could be faintly heard behind the music of the arcade games. She wanted nothing more than to pull on her armor, pick up a blaster, and take her stress out on the hapless cardboard Eels, but no. Today she would be an adult. She picked up the letter and stuffed it back in her messenger bag.

"Thanks, Harley."

"Tell Melville hello for me."

Before she left, she made sure to go out of her way to the laser tag room to tap the lava lamp. In the absence of the usual music, she could hear a low hum vibrating from inside. It rattled against its pedestal as she pressed her fingers to the warm glass. Several small globs of lava floated to the top, flashing as they changed shape. *Adults need luck too,* she thought to herself, then hurried out the door.

GRETCHEN WAITED until she got home before calling the phone number enclosed in the envelope. A cool voice answered before the dial tone sounded.

"Penelope Carsen."

The curt greeting caught Gretchen off guard, and she scrambled to find her words. "Um, hi. This is Gretchen Hollander. I'm calling because Great Aunt Elsie... I mean... I inherited a farm, I think..."

"Ah, yes. Gretchen. Can you meet tomorrow?"

"Yes, but I wanted to ask—"

"Great. I'll be at the Bromeliad Diner at noon. Looking forward to meeting you, Gretchen."

"But there's been a mistake—"

Click.

Gretchen lowered the phone. "I'll see you tomorrow, then..."

Gretchen's boss was none too happy when she requested the rest of the week off, but begrudgingly gave her the okay once she explained the situation. Gretchen hastily threw some clothes in a suitcase, crammed her study guides and textbooks on top, set her GPS, and hit the road.

4: DINER MEETING

THE BROMELIAD DINER, nestled between a barber's shop and an artsy boutique in the town square, bustled with activity. It overlooked the town square and a set of railroad tracks that cut across the street as if to keep an eye on the comings and goings of any who entered the town. Gretchen parked on the curb and walked toward the door. A couple of people gave Gretchen confused glances as she passed. She supposed the town didn't see many new faces.

Clang-a-lang-a-lang! A bell over the door rang as Gretchen stepped into the diner. Her fingers remained on the door handle as she surveyed the room. Large picture windows at the front lit the small interior and brown leather booths lined all of the walls, which were decorated with various species of bromeliads fastened to intricate wall fixtures. Above the tables and chairs which cluttered the floor, hung glass orbs containing clumps of Spanish moss. Most of the tables were occupied.

Several sets of eyes turned on her, freezing her into place. Forcing a smile, she offered an awkward wave. "Hi! I'm looking for Penelope Carsen."

A few returned to their meals, but one or two kept staring. Gretchen shuffled in place. "Um... I was supposed to meet her here about thirty minutes ago, but I got lost... Took a wrong exit." She chuckled nervously and ran a hand through her hair. "As I'm saying this, I'm realizing she probably left already."

With that, she lost their attention altogether. She cast her eyes about the room for a server, but with no luck. "I suppose I could ask someone in the kitchen." But her feet felt rooted to the floor. She wanted nothing more than to go back to her car and go home, but the thought of making a ten hour round trip for nothing was mortifying. She drew in a deep breath. As she took a step toward the kitchen, another door at the back of the room swung open, and a familiar tall, red-haired woman in a black turtleneck, black pants, and impressively high heels walked out. She caught Gretchen's eye and nodded.

"Nice to see you again."

Penelope beckoned her to a small table for two in one of the quieter corners of the room. A neat stack of papers towered over an empty coffee mug on its surface, its height causing Gretchen's stomach to twist. It all seemed so unnecessary. But she held her tongue as she slid into the opposite seat from the woman. A blue folder at the bottom of the stack poked out, and she caught the glittering emblem of a compass before Penelope tucked it into place. "What is all this?"

"Don't worry about it. I only need your signature on a few documents and then we need to discuss a few things."

"I don't know how to run a farm," Gretchen said.

Penelope waved a hand to flag down a waitress. "That's okay. I know plenty of people who can help you get started."

The waitress pulled a worn notepad from the pocket of her green apron.

"I'd like more coffee," said Penelope. "Gretchen, whatever you order is on me today."

"Coffee is fine. Listen—"

Penelope handed her mug to the waitress and cleared her throat. "Elsie typically sold some of her produce at the local farmer's market on weekdays. The rest, she sold to Roberto and I can put you in contact with him. If you want to continue that strategy this year, you'll want to start planting as soon as possible. I have a guy who can get some quality seeds for you to start out with—tomatoes, carrots, beets, spinach— but if you have anything else in mind, you'll have to look into it yourself."

"Um, wait, I have a question..." Gretchen tried cutting in.

But Penelope plowed on. "Cantaloupe would probably be a good thing to invest in this year. "It's a big property, so you will want to hire a helper or two."

At that moment, a man appeared at the edge of the table. Gretchen, relieved that Penelope had stopped talking, stared up at him. His scruffy beard took up most of his weather-beaten face, but she could tell from his eyes that he was smiling.

"Yer moving into Elsie's old place, huh?" he said, looming over her.

"Well, um, maybe," Gretchen said, shrinking back a little.

The facial hair parted as a wild, crooked-toothed grin spread over his face. "I'd be careful if I was you. Weird things are always happening there."

Penelope scowled. "Don't scare her, Billy. There is nothing wrong with Elsie's property. She was a sweet old woman, and she kept her place beautiful and neat."

"Oh, it's beautiful, alright," he said. "But that doesn't mean it ain't strange. I've lived at the house by Elsie's property my whole life. When I was ten, I was fishing in the retention pond, when my hook snagged on a big branch. I get a bit closer to untangle it, and... It ain't a branch. It's none other than the Loch Ness Monster."

Gretchen's eyes felt like saucers. "Could it have been an alligator?"

"A gator?" Billy wheezed with laughter. "Gators ain't that big. It was Nessie. I swear on my life!"

"I suppose Bigfoot met you for lunch afterwards," Penelope said.

"Mock me all you want—I saw it! I saw it with my own eyes!" Billy insisted, gesticulating wildly with his arms. "Hooked my fishing line right around one of its teeth!"

"Uh-huh. We know you did." Penelope picked up the stack of papers, and flipped through them, clearly done with the conversation. Billy's arms fell to his sides, and he huffed his disappointment.

"Have you seen anything since?" Gretchen asked.

Billy nodded. "Just last week, I saw a little one, wriggling beneath the water."

"A snake," Penelope said.

"I'll keep an eye out for any monsters," Gretchen said.

He nodded and plucked a napkin out of the dispenser on the table. Penelope protested when he took the pen from her hands, but he ignored her and scrawled out a number on the napkin.

"I live on the next property over. If anything ever happens, you can call me."

His heavy footsteps retreated, and the bell above the door clanged as he exited the restaurant.

"Is he always like that?" Gretchen asked.

Penelope shrugged. "You get used to it. Anyway," she took the first page from her stack and handed it to Gretchen. "All you need to do is sign here, and I can give you the keys. I need to talk to you about the property, but..." she cast a glance after Billy. "I don't want to be interrupted."

"What if I don't want to stay there?" Gretchen said.

Penelope's eyes narrowed in confusion. "Tonight?"

"No, I mean," Gretchen let out a nervous laugh, "what if I don't want the farm? What do I do?"

An odd expression that Gretchen couldn't quite place crossed the woman's face. Her brow furrowed as if caught between shock and panic. "You don't want... Well, you can always appraise it and then sell it." She blinked, her bafflement evident.

Gretchen capitalized on her speechlessness. "How do I do that?"

Penelope bit her lip and looked at the papers, and then at Gretchen. "I'll help you. But... I also need your help."

"How?"

She straightened her posture and collected herself. "Go through the house over the next few days and write down everything that's in there. Try to estimate how much it's worth. See what needs to be donated, what needs to be sold, and what needs to be thrown out. Then at the end of the week, I'll meet with you and we'll make a plan for clearing it out and selling the property."

"Oh, I'd be fine to donate everything," Gretchen began, but Penelope cut her off.

"Just look through everything."

"Okay," Gretchen conceded. Though she'd hoped to be able to take care of everything right then, she supposed it wouldn't hurt to stay a few days and help get the house in order. And maybe she'd be able to get some studying done in the peace and quiet of the farm.

Penelope thumbed through her stack of papers and pulled out a folder, though, not the one with the compass. She handed it to Gretchen.

"This will tell you everything you need for taking care of the llamas. They've been fed for the day, so you don't have to worry about that. I also put some maps in there to help you get around town."

She then fished through her purse and withdrew a set of keys, which clanked as they met the surface of the table. "These are for the house and the barn."

Before Gretchen could say anything, Penelope stood and picked up the rest of her stack. "If you will excuse me, I have a busy day ahead of me. I will see you in a week."

The bell over the door clanged as she left. Gretchen stared after her until the waitress returned and set two steaming mugs of coffee in front of her. "Will this be all, dear?"

"Yes. Can I go ahead and get the check? I guess I'm paying after all."

"Of course."

Gretchen tiredly wrapped her hands around one of the mugs, letting its warmth seep into her fingers. After a while, she took a pencil from her messenger bag and wrote on a napkin: *New schedule. 1. Catalog house. 2. Study.*

She finished off the first mug, and then the second before heading out to tackle the last leg of the journey.

THE COUNTRYSIDE BECAME MORE SLOPING the further Gretchen drove. Her car protested with tired groans as she prodded it up the last incline before Elsie's property came into view. An old, wooden sign greeted her as she followed a bend in the road. It should've read *Hildegard Farm* in its elegant, curving letters, but a few had faded or peeled, and the rounded stroke of the *d* was missing so that it read *Hil l Farm*. "Fitting," she said as she started up the steep driveway. "Hello, Hill Farm."

The little farmhouse was as quaint as the sign. It was one-story with whitewashed siding and a wrap-around porch. In the distance, a barn sat in the middle of a field, and further beyond that were more hills and a tree line, where the woods began. Gretchen slowed to take it all in.

Halfway up the driveway, she noticed the side of a wooden fence. She slammed on the brakes, threw her car into park, and stumbled out with a delighted gasp. Seven llamas stood at its edge, ears pricked forward, watching her intently. They ranged in color from creamy whites to dark browns. Some were spotted, and others freckled. A very large brown llama stood in the center, wearing an extremely serious expression on his long, narrow face—quite a feat for a creature with such a laughable appearance.

"You're so cute!" she exclaimed. "Hello! I'm Gretchen! I'm taking care of you this week!" she called. She waved and received a few barely perceptible tail wags in response. "Which one of you is Melville?" But as she approached, they turned and took off running over the hill. "Oops," she said. "I promise I'm not scary. We're going to be good friends."

Gretchen returned to her car and finished pulling it up to the house, where she parked beneath a carport in front of the garage. She hopped up onto the porch and came to the doorway. Keys jangled together as she unlocked the front door and pushed it open.

The living area looked as if it hadn't been vacant for long. A sofa and a couple of recliners huddled around a rug. The couch faced the far side of the room, which contained a fireplace. A bookshelf, crammed full of books, sat nearby. Their titles were still legible, even under the dust. *Twenty-thousand Leagues Under the Sea, Frankenstein, Pride and Prejudice, Moby Dick, Tom Sawyer...* So Elsie had been a fan of the classics.

Gretchen continued her exploration of the house. In the kitchen, countertops lined the walls, and an island stood in the middle. She opened a few doors and found a pantry, a bathroom, and the garage. When she peeked into the garage, she winced at the absolute mess inside and closed the door. *Nope. Too tired for that,* she thought.

A set of double doors on the opposite side of the kitchen revealed a dining room with a long oval table, but only two chairs. The way they huddled together caused a wave of sadness to well up inside of Gretchen, and she wondered if anyone else had lived here with Elsie. She couldn't recall anyone mentioning a husband at the funeral. Quietly, she closed the doors again.

Past the dining room and down the hallway, she found a laundry room, with a washer and dryer. Opposite it was the bedroom.

Gretchen rolled her suitcase to the floor by the bed and set it on its side. She tossed her messenger bag onto the mattress and stretched. "I suppose I should start cataloging everything," she said, absently slipping her phone from her pocket. She was surprised to find she still had cell service and typed out a quick message to Harley: *I'm here!*

She waited a few minutes.

No response.

With a sigh she wandered out to the living room, unsure of what to do or how to start. *A list,* she thought. *It's just a big list and I need paper and a pen.* The five hour drive began to weigh on her, and instead of searching for paper and a pen, Gretchen found herself sitting on the couch. Its cushions were hard and scratchy, but gravity prevented her from standing again. She checked her phone. No new messages lit the screen.

Gravity became more and more treacherous as she leaned to the side, and suddenly found herself sprawling vertically across the cushions. This position wasn't any more comfortable, yet her eyelids still drooped. As hard as she fought it, gravity won. She wouldn't ever remember falling asleep.

5: Hildegard Farm

NOT THE TEXT Gretchen hoped to wake up to. She rubbed the sore spot where her glasses had pressed into the side of her face and tried to shake the stiffness from her muscles. The curt nature of the message made her disinclined to complete Penelope's task, and she wondered what would happen if she packed up and went home before she arrived. But the thought of another long drive and returning to work right after caused her to go to the bedroom and fish a notebook, a pencil, and a granola bar from her messenger bag.

She made headings at the tops of several pages: *BEDROOM, LIVING ROOM, KITCHEN, GARAGE*. Then, she peeked into the closet in the corner of the room.

Dresses, sweaters, shirts, and pants hung neatly from hangers. Gretchen flipped to the *BEDROOM* page and wrote: *Clothes.*

"This is gonna be easy," she said to herself. She added "bed", "desk", and "lamp" to the list. "Easy and pointless."

She moved on to the living room. After taking note of each piece of furniture, she wandered over to the bookshelf. The colorful titles drew a smile to her face, and she debated whether or not to write each individual title. In the end, she jotted down "books" and left it at that.

A couple more long, low bookshelves lined the far wall, but unlike the first shelf, the books were all uniform and blank. Gretchen ran her fingers over the cracked spines of the old journals. She slid one off the shelf and brushed the dust off the brown leather cover. Paper whispered against paper as the thing fell open in her hands, revealing the faded pencil scrawl: *Hildegard Farm's Catalog of Creatures.* The handwriting matched that of Elsie's letter. She turned the page and found a note.

Dear Reader,

Hildegard Farm is home to a variety of species—all fascinating and worthy of appreciation. I have taken it upon myself to provide a guidebook for anyone who happens to share a love for the wonders of our world, no matter how small. This book is dedicated to you. Happy exploring,

Elsie

The other side held a hand-drawn map of the property. Gretchen found the road that led up to the house.

More drawings decorated the rest of the book. They were mostly animals—birds, mice, deer. She admired the detailed sketches on the yellowed paper and then came to an entry that described a rainy day investigation of a ditch. Aquatic invertebrates and flying insects took up most of the section. The tiny notes which intertwined the pictures recorded numbers of each species caught, natural history, and each of the life cycle stages Elsie had found that day. One particularly striking illustration depicted a heron standing in the water with a frog dangling from its beak. Gretchen couldn't help but wonder the fate of the frog.

A wide grin spread over her face when she turned to the next two pages, where a long, winding illustration of some kind of salamander took up the entire spread. It could've been an eel, had not two comically small sets of limbs dangled from its pectoral and pelvic girdles. Each limb sported three toes, and a goofy smile curved up the creature's face, making it look like the most amiable salamander in the world. Gretchen squinted at her great aunt's handwriting. *"Amphiuma tridactylum,"* she read. "Okay, I *have* to find one before I leave."

She closed the journal and slid it back on the shelf. When she picked up her list, she hesitated. Surely they couldn't be worth much. Surely it couldn't hurt to "forget" to pack a few with the other books. When she finished erasing, all that remained was a smudge of graphite.

Gretchen moved to the kitchen, took one look under the cluttered cabinets, and decided to try the garage. She grasped the rusted handle and gave a firm tug. The door opened with a scraping noise.

The sight of the garage made her stomach sink. Boxes upon boxes, stacked atop each other in haphazard mounds, took up most of the space. She stepped down onto the chilly stone floor and pulled the first grimy cardboard container she came to off one of the stacks. The flaps sent up a cloud of dust as she pulled them open, and the sight of yellowed papers greeted Gretchen. For a moment, a brief hope that she'd found more journals welled up in her, but it was dashed as she scanned the paper on top. Numbers and equations.

"Ugh, I've had enough math this week," she said, replacing the lid.

She crossed to the other side of the garage and found a few bicycles, tents, lanterns, and what looked to be climbing gear. Gretchen excitedly hopped over a dirty, old aquarium to pick up a large grappling hook. Its four, sharp points glinted in the afternoon light.

Gripping the rope, she gave the apparatus a couple of gentle test swings. The weight and the energy felt nice in her hands. "This doesn't need to be cataloged either, does it?"

The hook picked up momentum as it swung, as did Gretchen. Without thinking, she attempted to swing it in a wide loop. But the hook smashed right into a stack of boxes, toppling it. Gretchen winced and set the thing down. Her attention moved to the back of the garage.

Her heart skipped a beat.

Seven walkers with seven hooded cloaks draped over them were lined up in a row.

The monks.

Gretchen cast a furtive glance around the garage, half-expecting one of the tall figures she'd met at the funeral to step out from behind one of the mountains of boxes. But the space was empty. She made a mental note to check that all the doors and windows of the house were tightly shut and locked before she went to bed that night.

She glanced at her clipboard. Her scribbling hand-writing filled most of the space on the page.

"I should take a break."

The garage door had a pull handle on it, and with a grunt of effort, Gretchen got it to roll upward. Pale light poured in.

"Time to go exploring!" she announced. Leaving the checklist on top of a box, she set out.

Puffy white clouds obscured most of the sky, and Gretchen pulled her jacket a little closer around her. The air felt damp and chill as she surveyed the area, taking in the fields and the paddock, and the forest beyond, trying to determine the most likely place an amphiuma would be.

When she neared the llama paddock, she caught sight of the herd and waved. Seven sets of eyes watched her from the gate. One of them leaned toward the llama in the center and nuzzled its ear, as if passing along a secret. Gretchen gave up and lowered her hand. She continued onward, past the paddock to the fields beyond.

Wandering aimlessly, she followed along the plowed lines and wondered who could have made them. "Elsie climbed Everest," she said to a lone rabbit in a clump of grass. "Maybe she still plowed fields at a hundred years old."

The rabbit's nose twitched.

"Yeah," she agreed. "That's completely ridiculous."

She continued to wander the property until it became dark and the wind picked up. Shadowy clouds rolled overhead.

"Time to go back," she decided as she watched them scoot across the sky. She took a different path and eventually came to a ditch, which stretched toward the house. Gretchen knelt to examine it. The dank scent of muddy water met her nostrils and her nose crinkled.

Maybe it was the illustration of the ditch in the journal. Maybe it was the stillness of the water. But something about the ditch caused her to pause. Leaning over, she attempted to peer into the murky water. Her fingers hesitated, then plunged into the depths. The water ran up to her elbow by the time she found the bottom, and a shiver ran through her blood as she groped blindly through the unknown. Thoughts of toothy fishes, snakes, and amphiumas swam through her mind and she would've pulled away if not for the burning sense of curiosity that egged her on. Her hand squished and squelched through what she hoped was cold mud and algae, then wrapped around what felt like a gelatinous softball.

"Oh my gosh!" she exclaimed, withdrawing the

largest amphiuma egg she had seen in her entire life. Not that she had ever seen an amphiuma egg, but she could make out the shadow of a long embryo, coiled inside.

"This is freaking cool."

The farmhouse had an empty tank sitting in the garage. No landlord could tell her she couldn't have a pet. Gretchen dipped her bucket into the water, filling it almost to the brim. Ever so gently, she set the egg inside. Thunder rumbled overhead, and she made a beeline for the house, shoes squelching through the mud as she staggered under the weight of the bucket. By the time she reached the house, the wind had started to blow, and fat drops of freezing rain splattered against her skin.

The musty darkness of the garage brought relief from the cold and the wet. Gretchen felt around for a light switch, but with no luck. "Oh right... It's a pull switch in the middle of the room. Great..." Pain shot through her elbow when she bumped it into some large, unknown object, and a loud crash sounded as the thing toppled to the floor. She reached up and found the chain for the light and gave it a tug.

Click.

Dim yellow light spilled over the mess. She now clearly saw the bicycle she'd knocked over and the boxes it had crashed into.

"Oops."

Piles of old books, paper, and odd instruments lay strewn across the floor. She carefully picked around the junk to reach the aquarium she'd seen earlier. Hoisting it up under her arm, she carried it inside, to the bathroom. The bathtub knobs let out a metallic squeal as she ran the faucet as hot as it would go and left it to partially fill the tank.

After a few minutes of searching for a rag, she gave up and grabbed her toothbrush. She set to scrubbing —bearing down on the glass with the instrument until the grime came away. Though the work made her arm muscles scream in protest, she felt the anxieties which had plagued her mind all day begin to calm.

Scrtch, scrtch, scrtch. The rhythmic scrape of the bristles against the surface drowned out her thoughts. A couple hours slipped by and the tank started to look decent. Most of the caked mud had come loose, leaving only a few brownish streaks. At 1:00 AM, Gretchen set the tank on its stand and admired her work.

"I'll put you in your new crib and go to bed," she said to the egg.

The bucket sloshed as she propped it against the side of the tank. Then, gently so as not to damage the delicate thing, tilted it forward to slowly pour the water in. As the bucket got low, she reached in and scooped the egg into the palm of her hand and set it at the bottom of the tank. The muddy water made it difficult to see the finer details of the embryo, but she could see its long, coiled body twitching in its gelatinous little orb of a world.

"Sweet dreams," she said, then stood to go wash the mud from her arms.

Outside, the storm intensified. Gretchen burrowed beneath the unfamiliar blankets and tried to get some sleep. The howling wind caused the eaves to creak until she feared the whole roof would collapse on her. When she finally drifted off, she dreamed of wolves, chasing her through the dark.

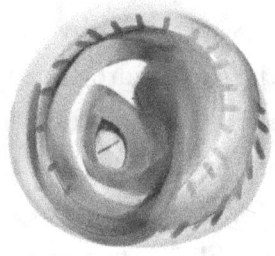

6: Breakdown

Sunlight spilled through the window and across Gretchen's bed, eliciting a small groan. "Why are there no curtains?" she said into her pillow.

It took a few minutes for her to convince herself to push off the blankets and roll to her feet. Without sparing a glance in the direction of the aquarium in the corner, she stumbled to the bathroom, feeling the stress creeping in. So many things had to get done today, and she felt qualified for exactly none of them. She frowned at the muddy toothbrush on the floor.

"Gross."

A finger would have to do. She picked up her tube of toothpaste and squeezed a sticky drop onto the end of her pointer finger. As she smeared the minty paste over her teeth, she ran through her to-do list. Penelope promised to come at two o'clock, so that left her the morning to split between studying and cataloging the farm equipment. She needed to take another practice exam, too. "But I can't do any of that if I'm hungry!" she told her reflection. "I'll go to the grocery store, get a toothbrush and food, and *then* start making a list of what's here. Then I can go through my books once Penelope leaves."

A few curls stuck out at odd angles, so Gretchen ran her fingers through them until they behaved. Once satisfied, she returned to the bedroom to retrieve her wallet and some clothes from her suitcase. But first, she wanted to see. Her glasses sat on the nightstand. As she slid them on, the world slid sharply into focus, and a motion in the corner of the room caught her newly corrected gaze.

Something stirred in the aquarium.

Gretchen slowly approached. The egg was gone. A thread-like creature with a giant head drifted in circles around the tank. She took in its glass-like body with awe. It had teeth, but no limbs. "You're not an amphiuma. You're some sort of eel, aren't you?" she said as its large, round eye stared back at her. "I will name you Neel."

Neel didn't protest.

"I'll bet you're hungry, Neel. I am too, so I'll go shopping for the both of us, and we can feast together while we wait for Penelope to show up!"

Gretchen pulled on a hoodie and some sneakers and searched around for her folder of maps. Once she located it, she broke her promise of waiting to eat with Neel and heated up a breakfast burrito before heading out to her car.

Wet gravel squelched into the mud beneath her feet. From across the field, the llamas watched her. Their heads turned to follow as Gretchen, keys and maps in one hand and steaming burrito in the other, battled with the lock on the car door. The heavily eyelash-ed stares unnerved her, and she was glad when she finally plopped into the driver's seat, where she finished off her breakfast.

With a little coaxing, the car flared to life. A new rattling noise accompanied the engine's usual coughs and splutters, but she drowned it out with the radio. The car picked up speed as it rolled down the sloped driveway, and Gretchen found herself frantically tapping the brake pedal for fear of skidding into the trees on the other side of the road. The vehicle jolted as it hit the asphalt, but held together. Gretchen checked her map again and drove on.

The radio cut out the further she got from Elsie's property. Beautiful stretches of woods and fields unfolded before Gretchen. She only passed one other house, sitting in a field. A couple miles down from the house, static crackled and the radio signal returned again. Gretchen slowed and peered out the left window. A little concrete building caught her attention. From the outside, it wasn't clear what it was exactly, but it looked official. The exterior was made of plain, even brick, with no signage, and only one narrow window, covered by blinds.

"Interesting," she said. The building wasn't marked on the map. "Very interesting."

The signal held until Gretchen reached the highway. She counted the number of songs that played as she sped down the black asphalt. After the fourth she sighed. "Four songs. I can't live here. Imagine having to drive this every time I need something," she said to herself. She'd have to drive even further if she needed to play laser tag, she thought grimly. And the closest laser tag game probably didn't have aliens or eels, and definitely didn't have Harley.

At last, she reached the supermarket. She pulled into a parking space beside a brown pickup truck with a bed that resembled the inside of Elsie's garage. Piles of boxes and junk were crammed together and loosely tied down with a couple of straps. Gretchen supposed her own car wasn't too out of place beside it. She locked her door and headed through the sliding glass doors.

Fluorescent lights caused her to squint as she entered the building. People bustled about, and the rattle of shopping carts mixed with the beeps from the checkout lines. Gretchen tried to orient herself as she secured her own cart. It seemed to be set up like any other supermarket, so she headed toward the back, in the direction she hoped she'd find the pet supplies aisle.

"I'll get Neel's stuff, and then groceries," she told herself.

Pet supplies were hidden away behind the lawn ornaments aisle, just as she expected. Tacky fish tank decor lay scattered haphazardly over the shelves. Gretchen picked up a ceramic tiki hut that looked big enough to house the eel, checked the price, and added it to her cart. Heaters and water filters lined the next section of shelves, but they were expensive, and Gretchen planned on letting Neel go at the end of the week anyway.

The smell of fish food met her on the next aisle. Brine shrimp, algae pellets, colorful flakes... Gretchen read the packages with a touch of frustration. She wasn't sure if Neel would even eat fish food. Something told her he wouldn't be overly impressed by the thin flakes or the tiny bits of shrimp. His sharp teeth glinted in her mind's eye and sent her wheeling away from the pet food aisle and in the direction of the meat section.

Packages of bright red meat lined the chilly shelves, and she had to wait for an old man to make his choice and move along so that she could get a closer look at the ground beef. She ended up dropping two half-pound packages in her cart.

"Alright! Now for *my* food!"

Gretchen went through her list and hunted down the groceries she needed for the week. She was debating pulling a carton of chocolate milk from the refrigerated section when footsteps approached.

"Hello, neighbor!" called a familiar, gruff voice. She turned to see Billy, a box of fishing tackle under one arm and a pack of beer under the other.

"Are you going to a lake?" she asked.

He chuckled. "Nah. I figured I'd hang around the retention pond this weekend and try to catch a photo of Nessie. Figure I can sell it to a magazine or somethin'."

"Sounds more fun than what I'm doing today," said Gretchen. "Penelope is coming to help me appraise the house."

"I don't envy you. Best of luck with that."

Gretchen checked the clock on her phone and frowned. "I have to get back. See you later!"

"Hey..." Billy put a large hand on her shopping cart before she could leave. A frown tugged at his lips, as if something were worrying him, and he was trying to put words to it. "I wouldn't be so quick to trust the Carsens if I were you. They're friendly enough, but they definitely have an agenda of their own."

Gretchen gave a bewildered nod.

"Alright. Take care," he said, releasing the cart. His boots thudded against the tile as he walked away.

Gretchen pulled open the glass door and set a

carton of chocolate milk in her cart, mulling over his words. Penelope had seemed abrupt, yes, and Edgar was almost overly kind, but nothing caused her to suspect they were doing anything other than helping carry out the last wishes of a friend. She wasn't sure how much stock she could put into his words anyway. He believed the Loch Ness Monster lived in the retention pond, after all. Despite her reasoning, she decided to keep an eye on Penelope when she arrived at the house.

She passed a few more aisles and came to a display full of school and office supplies. Glitter pens sparkled invitingly under the harsh fluorescent lights. Gretchen was examining a pack of kitten stickers when a box of spiral-bound sketchbooks caught her eye. They weren't anywhere near the quality of Elsie's books, but nonetheless, one of them ended up in Gretchen's cart along with the stickers and pens. She even remembered to pick up a new toothbrush.

THE HANDLES of the grocery bags dug into Gretchen's forearms as she made her way out of the store. Thoughts of restored circulation to her fingertips hurried her steps toward her car. She had to set her bags on the pavement to dig her key from her messenger bag, and then quickly transferred them into a pile in the passenger seat before sliding in herself.

She turned the key in the ignition, but nothing happened.

"No."

She tried again. Nothing.

"No!"

She forgot to undo her seat belt as she clambered out of the car, and struggled to untangle herself. Her car couldn't be dead. Not while she was stranded in the middle of nowhere, trying to get rid of a farm she didn't want.

The hood popped open when she pressed the button, and she surveyed the car's innards.

"Yep. That is the inside of a car," she said, poking at the wires and wishing she had watched what the mechanic did last time it broke down.

Gretchen leaned her forehead against a headlight and groaned.

"What are you doing?" said a familiar voice behind her.

She raised her head slightly as Billy approached. "I have absolutely no clue."

He chuckled. "Want help?"

"Do you work miracles?"

The man approached the car and took a good, long look at the engine, occasionally reaching out to poke something and mumble under his breath. Finally, he let out a low whistle, stood, and wiped his hands on his jeans.

Gretchen watched him anxiously.

"Yeah, I can fix this," he said.

The tension left her shoulders, and she pushed a stray lock of hair behind her ear. "Right now?"

Billy laughed. "Nah, I'll have to tow it. I need my tools." He moved to the truck Gretchen had seen earlier and rifled through the junk. He pulled a rusty bicycle out and set it on the pavement. "I can't give you a ride back to Elsie's. I'm carrying this stuff to sell it, and the truck's full up. But you could probably use a ride home."

"Thank you," she said, wondering how in the world she was going to balance her groceries.

Billy held his hand out for the key. "I'll pick it up on my way back."

As soon as he left, Gretchen walked back into the store, where she bought a small ice chest, a bag of ice, some thick wire, and a pair of pliers. Before too long, her new bicycle had an ice chest wired to the front of the handlebar, and the non-perishables dangling in their bags from each handle. She patted her car's bumper, and then wobbled her way out of the parking lot.

The road was relatively well-kept, and it didn't take too long for Gretchen to get the hang of balancing her ridiculous contraption. She picked up speed as the ground sloped downward, and soon came to the highway. Though the day was cool and cloudy, it wasn't long before sweat beaded on her forehead, her muscles became sore, and she had to stop to rest. She leaned her forehead against the handlebars.

"Four songs. This is a four-song road," she panted, wishing she'd stayed at the grocery store.

She allowed herself a few minutes of rest before pushing on. The rest of the ride became a game of stop and go. Occasionally, cars passed, but she was too chicken to stick her thumb out at them. By the time she reached Elsie's street, her shirt was drenched, and she felt woozy. "This. Is. A. Sixteen. Song. Road," she gasped.

Blue lights flashed ahead. Gretchen skidded to a halt outside the unmarked building, causing the contents of the ice chest to slosh, and the bike to tilt dangerously to one side. She planted one foot firmly on the ground to keep herself from careening sideways into the pavement. Bright yellow police tape surrounded the front of the building and a couple of investigators surveyed the scene. They were dressed in the county's khaki uniforms and had an air of frustrated amusement about them.

"What happened here?" Gretchen called to one of them, a woman who appeared to be taking a water break by the patrol car.

The woman scratched her head. "We're not sure! Someone broke in during the night, but the security cameras didn't catch them."

"It looked fine this morning. Did no one notice until now?" Gretchen asked.

The investigator approached Gretchen. To her great relief, she offered up her water bottle. "Did you notice anyone suspicious?"

Gretchen shook her head as she gulped down the cold water. After draining half the bottle, she handed it back. "I didn't see anyone. Is it a robbery?"

"Yes and no. The only things touched were a few old dusty files, but nothing seems to be missing. Probably kids pulling a prank, but the owner and the workers are pretty upset."

"Did you dust for fingerprints?"

"Yeah. Nothing except a bit of what looks like drool on the handle of a filing cabinet. They must've had a dog with them."

"That's so weird," Gretchen said. "I have to get back before my groceries spoil, but good luck with the investigation!"

Gretchen pedaled as fast as she could the rest of the way to the farm. Sweat dripped from her entire body when she finally pulled into the driveway. To her dismay, a sleek black car sat parked in front of the garage. Penelope. She glanced at the time on her phone. Forty minutes late. She was painfully aware of how disheveled she looked as she opened the front door.

Penelope sat in one of the recliners in the living

room, legs neatly crossed, a book in one hand, and a cup of tea in the other. She didn't look up from her book as Gretchen dropped her grocery bags in the entrance.

"I'm so, so sorry. I know I'm late, but my car broke down and Billy had to use his truck, and—"

"Take a seat," Penelope said in a tense voice.

Gretchen obediently sank into the second recliner, wincing as her sweaty body met the thin fabric of the chair. After a few moments of awkward silence, Penelope shut the book and set it on the end table beside her. She straightened her posture and leveled her stare at Gretchen. Gretchen couldn't help but notice how perfect she looked again. Like yesterday, she was dressed from head to toe in black, and donned impossibly high heels. Gretchen's own feet ached at the thought. She, herself, probably would have tripped and broken a bone if she tried walking in them for even a nanosecond.

"Do you have any idea what I've been through today?" the other woman asked, folding her hands neatly in front of her.

Gretchen shook her head.

"Chaos," said Penelope, emphasizing the word. "I have been through *chaos* this morning. I had to leave the chaos to come meet you, and then you were late. Have you at least cataloged everything?"

"No," said Gretchen, bewildered.

Penelope stood and pinched the bridge of her nose. "I'm beginning to think you're not cut out for this."

Gretchen also stood and wandered over to the cooler to hide the scowl contorting her features. What the hell was going on? Penelope had said she could take her time deciding. What changed? Billy's warning played over in her mind. She bent to open the lid and pulled out her sack of groceries.

"You need to figure out what you want, Gretchen. I can't let the house sit here, empty. If you can't handle the job, I will have to find a replacement."

Gretchen ignored her and placed the items in the refrigerator, hoping they hadn't spoiled.

"Do you know what you want?" Penelope pressed.

"You said I had the whole week to think things over."

Penelope put her face in her hands. "I did, didn't I?"

"Yes," said Gretchen.

"Forgive me. You have no idea how crazy this morning has been," she groaned. "I have to get back to work, but *please* keep working on that catalog. It's a great help to me."

Gretchen followed her to the door to see her out.

Before she left, she paused on the doorstep and looked out to the field. "Also, you might want to ask around about your llamas. Looks like the fence is down and the paddock is empty," Penelope said.

"Oh," said Gretchen, a wave of exhaustion washing over her.

Penelope drove away, leaving Gretchen to stand and stare dumbly at the empty paddock. She spent the rest of the afternoon wandering the farm and calling for the herd until she was hoarse. The neighbors weren't any help. But the llamas appeared to have vanished into thin air.

Defeated, she returned to the house and had a good, long cry. When she finally dried her puffy eyes, she realized how late it had become. She sank into one of the recliners, but then leapt up again. Her hands tugged at her hair as she remembered. "Oh no. Neel! I'm a horrible eel mom!"

She ran to the kitchen and yanked open the refrigerator door. Cool air sent a shiver through her as she searched the shelves for where she'd hidden Neel's dinner. Finally locating the package of ground beef, she carried it back to the bedroom.

Neel was waiting. His long, glassy body waved languidly as he watched her with his sharp, hungry eyes. Their focus unnerved her.

Plastic crinkled as Gretchen peeled the protective film back from the foam package of beef. The slimy, ground-up square of red meat squished between her thumb and forefinger, finding its way underneath her fingernails as she pinched a large chunk from the square. She made a face. "This is why I never cook," she said to the little creature. He wriggled impatiently, his nose repeatedly bumping against the glass.

"Hold your horses, buddy! Food is on the way."

She lifted the lid and shook the piece of beef from her fingers. It fell into the water with a *plop!* that sent droplets splashing out of the tank. Neel snapped at the meat with a voracity that was shocking for his size. He scarfed it down and looked at Gretchen, mouth opened as if expecting more. She eyed the lump in his stomach.

"Why don't you work on that for now? I'll give you more at breakfast."

Gretchen went to wash her hands, then slowly prepared for bed as she ran through her notes about Neel.

Neel definitely wasn't an eel. He wasn't an amphiuma, either. It bothered her that she still couldn't figure out what species he was. His eyes seemed far too calculating for a fish, but perhaps they only seemed that way because of their placement on his head. "If it's new to science, I guess I'll describe it." She cast an anxious glance at the books on the floor before turning out the light.

7: The Monks

Near ten o'clock that night, Gretchen awoke and found that she couldn't fall back to sleep. Her entire body throbbed from the day's impromptu bike ride, and she tossed and turned, trying to find a position that didn't make her want to die. Finally, she decided that if her body wasn't going to cooperate, she might as well engage her brain and get some studying in. "And what better to help me study than a nice glass of chocolate milk?" she said, swinging her aching legs out of bed.

The floorboards creaked under her socked feet as she made her way to the kitchen. She poured a glass of chocolate milk, and then sat at the table, watching the lightning through the thin, checkered curtains which hid the window. Between the flickers, a softer flash of light caught her eye. She stood and squinted past the water droplets that dotted the glass panes.

"Why must we check again? We already got data."

"Yes. We have to be sure. We have to eliminate them all."

Gretchen felt her soul plummet through her feet. The voices sounded angry and muted at the same time. She whirled around, searching wildly for their source, but the room was empty. Dark shadows loomed, and she could no longer remember what furniture sat where, making every silhouette seem sinister. The wood grains of the table scratched against her fingertips as her hand slid across the surface, searching for something, *anything*, to use as defense.

Her pinky brushed the spine of one of her textbooks. She clasped her hands around the entire stack, drew it to the edge of the table, then picked it up and gripped it in front of her like a shield. Her ears strained, seeking out the voices again. Every creak of the floorboards now felt like a shrieking alarm beneath her feet as she crept down the hallway.

She arrived at the dining room doors and pressed her ear against the wood of the one on the right. It took a moment for her to register anything other than the pounding of her own heart in her ears, but then, low murmurs seeped past its frantic beat. It was the monks. Gretchen was sure of it. Taking a deep breath, she tightened her grip on her books, ready to whack someone if need be, and pulled open the door.

The stack tumbled to the ground.

Seven llamas stood gathered around the table, apparently in a meeting. They poured over clusters of documents, but as the door creaked open, they paused in their discussion to stare at her. Gretchen stared back. And shrieked.

She must've looked weak in the knees, because a couple of llamas moved to both her sides and pushed their shoulders under her elbows in support. They guided her to the table, where the largest of the herd turned his dark, heavily-lashed gaze on her.

"Welcome, Gretchen. I suppose that as the new farmer, it's only fitting that you attend this war council."

"War council?" she said, faintly.

He nodded.

Another llama beside him cleared his throat. This one had dark circles around his eyes, resembling glasses. "Judging by Elsie's notes, and the notes from the lab, invasion is imminent within the next two weeks."

"The next two weeks?" Gretchen repeated hollowly.

"We don't have an exact date, but yes," he said. "There is a ninety-seven percent chance it will occur in the next two weeks." The llama tapped one of the documents with a cloven hoof.

Gretchen looked at it, and then back at the llama. "Why can you talk?"

The question drew a few chuckles from around the table, and the head llama's lips curled into a llama's version of a smile. He nudged a couple of documents away with his nose. "This is a good time for a break. Let us introduce ourselves, and then we will tell you our story."

The llama with the eye circles smiled at Gretchen. "My name is Einstein."

A nearly black llama beside him flicked her ears. "Shelley."

The next llama had very pronounced ear tufts. He introduced himself as Twain. Next came Brontë and Austen. Then Verne.

Gretchen turned to the head llama. "And you're...?"

"Call me Melville."

Gretchen opened her mouth and closed it a few times. "Could you always talk?"

Melville shook his head. "No, we were gifted with speech when we were very young. We were chosen before we were even weaned from our mothers' milk."

"Chosen by whom?" she asked.

All the llamas closed their eyes and let out a low hum.

"The ones from above. They carried us away, gave us intelligence, and then brought us back."

"And the invasion?"

"Horrible monsters from beyond the stars. We're sworn to defeat them."

Gretchen nodded numbly. "So let me repeat this back at you so that I know I understand."

Melville returned the nod.

"You used to be normal llamas," she began.

"Mhm," said Melville.

"You got abducted by aliens and now you're super smart," she continued.

"That's it," the llama said with a great amount of patience.

"And last night, you broke into a science lab to steal documents pertaining to a possible alien invasion."

Melville turned to the others and exclaimed, "She's got it down perfectly!"

The others wiggled their ears happily.

Gretchen's hands found her temples. "Oh my gosh, I think I've lost it."

"What?" all of the llamas said at the same time.

Gretchen let out a giggle, which turned into a laugh, which turned into a wild cackle. She laughed, and laughed, and kept laughing as the startled creatures looked on. "I've lost it! Gone off the rails! Completely bonkers!" She stood and started to pace, no longer feeling the soreness in her legs. "Mom keeps saying that I've been studying too hard and not getting enough sleep!"

"What do you mean by that?" asked Shelley, a note of offense clear in her voice.

But Gretchen kept pacing. "This is too much, this is too much..."

The llama heads followed her back and forth, back and forth, until finally, she whirled to face them. "So, why'd they return you? The aliens. Why would they make you smart and then put you back?"

Awkwardness settled over the room. One of the llamas coughed, and another turned away bashfully.

"They became annoyed with our intelligence," said Brontë.

"They didn't want us," Einstein chipped in.

"We were abandoned," said Verne.

"But in our darkest hour, Elsie found us," Melville said with a sage bow. "She found us, named us, and cared for us."

"Well... That's... good?" Gretchen said, unsure of how to respond.

"It's amazing," said Melville. "Elsie was the best thing that could've happened to us."

"Wow," said Gretchen. She put her hands to her head again. "So... What was it like in space?"

The llamas exchanged glances.

"We were young llamas, *crias*, so it's hard to recall everything, but the lights were so bright," the tufted-eared llama, Twain, piped up. His eyes grew wide as he spoke. "But the aliens... Now, *they* are hard to forget. Tall cyclopes with dazzling white skin."

Shelley cut in. "They brought us food, toys, and books. Anything we ever could've wanted. However, it came at a price."

Austen took over. "We were poked and prodded with needles, tested and pushed to our limits, and worst of all..." she shuddered, "thrown into pits with our nemeses!"

"You have a nemesis?"

"Many," Melville spoke up as emotion overtook his friend. "Horrible creatures with gnashing teeth. They are a ruthless species with no qualms about killing and devouring the innocent, and they're headed this way." His expression became grave. "We were put here to defend the Earth from their inevitable invasion."

Gretchen nodded faintly. "And when are they getting here?"

Melville smiled. "That's what we're meeting to determine tonight."

"We need more data!" said Einstein in a pleading tone.

Melville sighed and seemed to cave. He caught Gretchen's eye again. "Would you like to come help us collect it?"

"Um... sure?" said Gretchen. She felt that was the right answer.

Melville's smile widened. "Excellent. Go get dressed and then meet us out front."

She threw several glances over her shoulder as she walked down the hall to make absolutely certain that she wasn't crazy. As she walked, she caught glimpses of the herd, filing out the door as if they'd done it a hundred thousand times before.

"Neel," she said, as soon as the bedroom door clicked shut behind her. "You'll never believe what just happened."

Neel showed no sign of surprise.

8: Break-In

Dressed in her hoodie and jeans from earlier, and with her messenger bag slung over her shoulder, Gretchen headed toward the porch. Her mind still reeled. A big part of her feared that she'd hallucinated the whole encounter. But as she stepped out the front door and onto the porch, the herd was waiting for her. They stood around a wagon, tails eagerly wagging.

"Hop in!" said Verne, nodding at it.

"You want to pull me?" she said, her face scrunching slightly as she noticed the seven walkers, stacked inside the wagon.

"Of course! It will be faster."

"Where are we going?" she asked, even though she had a strong hunch.

"We're going down the road to collect more data on the invasion," said Melville. "It shouldn't take long, especially with you riding."

Even in the darkness, Gretchen caught the glint of a hook hanging on a rope around his neck. She eyed the walkers again. "I'm not going to fit with those."

"We can't leave them," said Verne. What if we're seen?"

"Calm down, worrywart," teased Shelley. "We can leave them behind. We've never been caught."

Gretchen took the awkward contraptions out and set them in the grass. She stepped into the cart and made herself as comfortable as she could in the pile of cloaks. Twain checked to make sure she was situated and then walked forward. He fell into step beside Verne. Though the wheels rumbled against the pavement of the driveway, Gretchen could hear their high voices. She listened to them banter as they set a brisk pace.

"Doesn't this make you want to take off and see more of the world?" Verne said.

Twain hummed. "As long as we have a map. I don't like not knowing where we're going."

"No fun!" Shelley sang, zipping past them.

Melville suddenly appeared at the side of the cart. "I, for one, would love to see everything Elsie saw."

One of the cloaks became wrapped around Gretchen's foot as she shuffled around to face him. "You really miss her."

Melville nodded sadly.

"We all do," Verne said.

Before too long, they came to the concrete building off the side of the road. They left the wagon in a stand of bushes and approached the front door. Gretchen watched, intrigued as Melville leaned forward, pushed his hook around the door handle, then pulled it open with ease. She raised her eyebrows, impressed, giving him a small pat on the nose as she followed the herd into the building.

She found herself in a dark hallway. One of the llamas nuzzled a switch on the wall, and with an electric *pop!*, lights flared to life, revealing a door on either side of a short hallway.

"What is this place?" she breathed.

"A science lab," said Austen.

"Yeah, but who works here?"

"The aliens left it for us, but now it's owned by humans," explained Verne.

Gretchen nodded, even though the story made no sense. She pointed to the door behind them. "What's that?"

"The office," said Twain.

"What about that?" she asked, pointing to another door at the very end of the hall.

He frowned. "We don't go there."

A soft scraping sound caused everyone to wince as Melville succeeded in placing his hook around the handle of the door in front of them.

"And what's here?"

"You'll see," said Twain.

Hinges creaked softly as it opened, and they entered a dark room, lit only by the glow of screens and consoles. Little green and red lights flashed rhythmically, in tune with the steady beeps and whirs and hums of the various equipment lining the walls of the room. Melville approached the largest screen, which displayed a map of the area. It reminded Gretchen of the maps weather forecasters used to track storms. At the moment, green pixels, which must have represented clouds, covered most of the area in large patches.

"What is this place?" she asked in a hushed whisper as she tried to make sense of the map on the screen.

"They're tracking our enemies for us," said Austen.

"For you? Then why are we sneaking in?"

"Oh, they don't know they're doing it," said Melville. He watched the blinking screen intently. "They think they're tracking a weather phenomenon. Alien technology is very similar to radar."

Gretchen looked over the screen again, but could find nothing to indicate any abnormality other than clouds. She glanced over her shoulder and found the rest of the herd focused as hard as Melville. She decided her help was not needed and moved to examine the different instruments scattered around the room.

A set of five walkie talkies sat on a countertop over a collection of computer hard drives. Gretchen picked one up and pressed the call button, but only static came through. She set it back on its charging port.

A door on one wall led to another, much smaller room. After a bit of searching, she found a light switch and flicked it on. The incandescent bulb overhead hummed to life, shedding light on the black, metal filing cabinets that filled the room. Gretchen tugged on the nearest handle. Locked. However, one of the lower drawers didn't seem to be all the way shut. It easily slid open when she pulled. Manila file folders filled the entire drawer.

One, which stuck out a little higher than the others, caught her eye. She tugged it out of the drawer. *The H.I.LL. Project.* Gretchen flipped it open and fumbled as a small slip of paper fluttered to the floor. She bent to pick it up.

Dear Professor,

The llamas are beginning to exhibit an understanding of the English language far beyond the typical understanding of dogs or parrots or ravens. This morning, 001 said my name. We will be administering the second dose of the serum today. We will keep you updated.

—Elsie

Shock jolted through Gretchen's body as she stared at the now-familiar signature. She glanced over her shoulder where Melville and the others were still watching the screen. Experimentation by some kind of scientist with some kind of serum made more sense than alien abduction, but still... How would they not know?

Without taking her eyes off the herd, Gretchen removed the contents of the folder and replaced them with her test prep workbook from her messenger bag. She rejoined the llamas in the control room.

"The skies are still clear!" whispered Einstein excitedly. "Perhaps they've found a new place to bother."

"Einstein is afraid of them," said Shelley, practically rolling her eyes at Gretchen.

"And you're not?" Brontë asked with teasing amusement.

Shelley put her nose in the air. "The sooner we get this over with, the better."

Melville finally took a step back. The others copied him. Even Gretchen found herself following his lead as he turned to face the herd and cleared his long throat. "We have all the data we need for tonight."

A cheer went up.

AFTER MAKING sure everything was exactly how they'd found it, aside from the swapped file, Gretchen and the herd headed for the exit and stepped into the night. The waning moon now peeked through the clouds, throwing a weak swath of moonlight across the grass as they made their way to the bushes where the cart was hidden.

They'd almost made it, when the much brighter beam of a flashlight cut across the lawn.

Gretchen and the herd instinctively froze. A security guard appeared from behind the building. He stopped in his tracks, staring at the odd bunch before him.

"Hey!"

Adrenaline coursed through Gretchen's veins as she broke into a run and pushed through the bushes.

"Stop right there!" he called.

But Gretchen kept running. Branches snagged at her clothes and her skin, leaving behind leaves in her hair. The herd pelted through as well, though, a loud thud told her that at least one of them decided to jump over the scraggly branches.

As soon as she reached the cart, she vaulted over the side and crashed to its floor. Twain slipped into the harness and took off before she could even sit up. When she finally managed to right herself, she peeked over the edge of the cart and caught sight of the guard, still shouting after them.

They didn't slow down until they'd crossed the road and his shouts could no longer be heard. The llamas panted, but didn't stop to rest.

The rest of the trek back to Hildegard Farm flew by in a blur. The wheels of the cart rattled along the empty road, and the cloven hooves of the herd pattered against the asphalt. Gretchen barely remembered arriving, and sure as heck didn't remember inviting the llamas into the house, but they all soon found themselves in the living room.

"What a rush!" Gretchen cried, hopping up on the couch and bouncing a few times. The springs squealed under her weight as she jumped. Verne attempted to climb up with her, and when she tried to help him up, they both tumbled to the ground, giggling.

"This feels like something straight out of a spy movie!" she laughed.

"We've never seen a spy movie," said Austen.

"We've never seen a *movie*," Shelley corrected.

Gretchen sat up on her elbow. "What?! No! You've never watched a movie? Not even with the aliens?"

Heads shook.

Gretchen stood up. "Wait here. I have a few downloaded on my laptop. You *have* to watch one with me tonight!"

She ran back to the bedroom, blew a kiss to Neel, and grabbed her laptop. The llamas watched her curiously as she plugged the device into the wall and set it on the coffee table.

"What do we do?" asked Brontë as Gretchen selected one of the movies.

"Make yourselves comfortable, sit back, and watch," she said, turning the volume up. The llamas settled into a small heap, nuzzling each other and watching the title fade in on the small screen. Gretchen sat back, and at an invitation from Melville, leaned into his side. Snuggled in the warm wool of the llamas, she passed out before the movie even started.

9: PRISCILLA

THE NEXT MORNING found Gretchen sitting cross-legged on a pillow in the middle of Elsie's bedroom floor, a circle of open textbooks surrounding her. Her head spun. She must've gotten a total of four hours sleep, but the headache was nothing compared to how sore she felt, all over her body. She regretted sleeping on the floor and the muscles in her back screamed as she poured over the books.

Three lay open around her. All she had to do was turn a little to be able to read each one. She was quite proud of her system. One of the books lay open to the study tips chapter, one to the "L" section of the index, and one lay open to a cute picture of an iguana for motivation. Gretchen drew in a deep breath and attempted to expel all thoughts of talking llamas, but to no avail. "I'm not crazy. That really did happen last night," she told herself for the eighth time that day.

When she'd woken earlier, the herd was gone. She'd spotted them in the distance through the open front door and assumed they'd gone in search of breakfast. But, as the hours wore on, she'd begun to doubt her own memory. What if it had all been some exhaustion-induced dream?

She swiveled to the index. The tip of her finger traced smooth, glossy paper as she ran down the list, murmuring the animal names under her breath. "*Lacerta, Lagomorpha... Lama glama.* Page 215."

Thumbing to the indicated page, she scoured the section devoted to llamas. It was disappointingly small. "*Lama glama,* or the domesticated llama, is a part of the camel family, Camelidae. They originate from South America." *No mention of their use in science experiments, and definitely no mention of any tendencies toward getting abducted by aliens,* Gretchen thought. She bit her lip and turned a few pages to find a broader overview of Camelidae. All she found were taxonomic diagrams, showing that camelids belonged to the order Artiodactyla, even-toed ungulates who walked on the very tips of their toes.

She was interrupted as the herd filed in through the bedroom door. Gretchen's uncertainty fell away at the sight of their goofy smiling faces. "Hello, every-one!" she said, snapping the book in front of her shut.

"Hello, Gretchen," they greeted her, tails wagging.

Einstein knelt beside her. "How's the studying going?"

"About as well as expected after staying up all night," she giggled.

"Maybe take a break, then. Food and a nap usually helps me when I'm tired," he said. The others murmured their approval. Shelley and Verne nuzzled her to her feet.

"Okay! I get the point!" she laughed, reaching out to rub their noses.

"What is this?"

All the merriment was gone from Melville's tone. He had wandered to the back of the room and now stood beside Neel's tank, glaring at the eel with what Gretchen could only describe as hatred burning in his eyes. Neel glared back.

"That's Neel! He's my pet!" she said, moving to stand by the tank.

The other llamas gathered around, curiously peering past her. Small gasps went through the herd.

"Get rid of it," said Melville.

"Uh, no," Gretchen said, gently pushing him back. "He's mine. I hatched him, and there are no rules to say I can't have a fish in the house."

Melville blinked. "Fish?"

"Yeah. He looks a bit like an eel. He's probably some sort of fish. Definitely not an amphiuma."

Melville laughed. And kept laughing. The rest of the herd laughed too.

"Alright, everyone. Out of my room." Gretchen gave Melville another weak shove toward the door, but he resisted.

"You can't be serious. You can't keep that thing as a pet."

"Get *out!*" grunted Gretchen, smacking his neck.

A knock came from the front door of the house, freezing everyone in place. Gretchen and Melville exchanged a glance.

"*You* can't be in here!" she cried. "Penelope already hates my guts!"

"Who's Penelope?" asked Einstein.

"Out! Leave through the back door so she doesn't see you!" Gretchen said.

In a haze, she guided the herd around piles of dirty clothes, all the way to the back of the house as the knocking at the front became increasingly insistent. She pulled the door open and hurried the llamas through, one at a time. After locking the door, she hurried to the front of the house.

Gretchen attempted peering through the peephole, but her glasses scraped against the door and were pushed crooked across her face.

"I know you're in there!"

The voice didn't belong to Penelope. Gretchen opened the door and was greeted by the most pinched frown she had seen since Great Aunt Elsie's funeral. "Gretchen Hollander?" the woman said without preamble.

"Um, yes, hi. That's me. You're my cousin."

The woman's frown grew, if possible, more pinched. "I don't remember meeting you, but yes. Priscilla Snyder." She waited a moment before taking a step toward Gretchen. "Are you going to invite me in?"

In a daze of bewilderment and sleep deprivation, Gretchen stepped back and let her inside. Priscilla stormed to the middle of the living room, then stopped to wait. A mild headache set in as Gretchen shut the door.

"Can I get you anything to drink? Water? Chocolate milk?"

"That won't be necessary, I don't intend to stay." She looked Gretchen up and down, disdain etched in her face. "Who are you?"

Gretchen blinked. "Uh... I'm Gretchen?"

Priscilla's glare hardened. Gretchen decided that if she were ever forced to choose between being trapped in a room with Priscilla or in a room with a tiger, she'd pick the tiger. "Who are you to Elsie?" her cousin demanded.

"I don't know," Gretchen sighed, rubbing her face. "I think I only met her once, and I was really little and don't remember much."

With a huff, Priscilla turned and made a sweep

around the room, surveying the couch, the end tables, the lamp, the bookshelves... She ran her fingertips over the surface of the bookshelf, then examined them. "This farm was supposed to be mine. I've been dreaming of turning it into a bed and breakfast for years," she said.

"Why this particular farm?" Gretchen asked, eyes narrowing in suspicion. Did she know about the talking llama phenomenon? Nothing about her cousin's demeanor betrayed whether she knew about Melville or the others. In fact, Gretchen was willing to wager she didn't.

Priscilla crossed her arms. "Because my mother always told me that Great Aunt Elsie promised to leave it to our family. Why did she leave it to you? You're not even from a farming family!"

Gretchen shrugged. "I don't know."

"Have you ever even set foot on a farm before this week? You should be planting now—no—a week ago. And the fence is hanging wide open. Elsie's llamas are roaming everywhere. I saw one walking down the street last night!"

"Was it dressed in a long, hooded cloak and using a walker?"

"Oh, sure. It's all a big joke to you! This was supposed to be my future."

She busied herself with straightening the framed photographs on the wall.

"You're right," said Gretchen.

"What do you mean?"

"I'm not a farmer. I don't know why Elsie left the farm to me, and I'm not equipped to take care of it. You seem to know what you're doing. You should have it."

Priscilla's eyes widened and her face became a little less pinched. "What?"

Gretchen stepped beside her and wiped a streak of dust off the top of the shelf. "I'm going to vet school in the fall. I'm hardly going to have the time to manage this place." She picked up a photograph of Elsie and wiped the glass with the hem of her t-shirt. Setting the frame back on the bookshelf, she turned to Priscilla, who was watching her every movement. "Why don't we set up a meeting with Penelope and get this straightened out? I already signed some papers, so we'll probably have to sign a few more. I'm not sure how it all works."

It was as if a sheet of ice had melted. A wide smile spread over her cousin's face, and she hastily tucked a strand of hair behind her ear and cast a glance around the room, as if unsure of what to do with herself. "You mean it?"

"Yeah!" Gretchen said. "What am *I* going to do with a *farm*? And plus, you need it."

Priscilla's expression iced over again.

"What do you mean, I *need* it? I'm not asking for

charity," she said in clipped tones. "I will gladly pay whatever price you ask."

Gretchen put her hands up. "Whoa, I didn't mean it that way. You need it for your business."

Priscilla nodded curtly, though the anger didn't fade from her eyes.

"Why don't we get in touch with Penelope, and work it all out through her?"

"Yes. I think that is best," agreed Priscilla.

Gretchen exchanged contact information with her and saw her out of the house. As soon the door closed behind her, she sagged against it with relief.

The weight which had been hanging over her for the past few days lifted and was replaced by a light and airy sense of relief. "Priscilla will take over! She's older and more experienced and won't burn this place to the ground." Gretchen waltzed into the kitchen to pour herself a celebratory glass of orange juice. She carried it to the bedroom and grinned widely at Neel. "And then I can focus on studying, and maybe even fix my car with the money!"

The eel hovered in place, watching her.

"Don't worry. I'll return you to the place I found you before I leave. You'll be free to go about your eel life."

She stooped to pick up her books and caught sight of a corner of the classified file sticking out from her messenger bag. Maybe she should've mentioned the llamas to Priscilla. Setting aside the books, she picked up the file and opened it to the first page. *The Highly Intelligent Llama Project.* Her lips twitched as she read. Someone had a sense of humor.

The first few pages contained a list of numbers that corresponded with descriptions and photographs of young llamas. Her smile widened. The herd's baby pictures.

"Well," she murmured to herself, "alien abduction did seem rather far-fetched."

Behind the llama profiles, she found another note to the Professor from her great aunt.

Dear Professor,

I am sorry to hear that you can no longer care for your herd, but I am glad to take them off your hands. It may be more convenient for everyone this way. Long ago, Owlen and I determined that Hildegard Farm covers most of the affected area. We considered buying the neighboring tracts of land to ensure that if and when the situation spreads, the owner of the farm has full control of the properties, but we never found the funds to do so.

Thank you for helping me find a solution to manage the situation while still keeping it a secret. It would be a shame to lose something we know so little about. However, I feel comforted knowing that the herd is ready for disaster. I know I will not be around when things go south, but I have made progress in selecting a new farmer to take over when I am gone.

Take care and rest assured that I will look after the llamas.

—Elsie

Gretchen's heart thumped behind her ribs as she closed the file. *Selecting a new farmer.* Elsie had selected Gretchen. Some ominous threat had been hanging over the farm for years and Elsie selected Gretchen to deal with it. *Why?* She shoved the file back into her bag. Elsie had made a mistake, and she refused to let that mistake ruin her good mood.

THE REST of the day passed quickly. Gretchen flipped through her study materials, and at one point, dozed off. When she woke, she heated up a burrito and decided to visit the herd. She didn't see them in the field as she stopped by the barn to pick up some hay for them. At last, she spotted the llamas on the far side of the field and headed toward them.

"Dinnertime!" Gretchen called, stepping into the paddock, a small bale of alfalfa under each arm. She tried to kick the gate shut, but missed. It wasn't like it mattered anyway.

She found the herd in front of the stables, gathered around Melville and talking in hushed voices. The conversation halted, and seven heads turned toward her as she approached. Anxiety prickled in her mind worse than the grass prickled at her side. She had a sneaking suspicion they weren't talking about the weather.

"Hey!" she panted, setting the bales down and

trying to act like she didn't notice the way they glared at her. "I brought your food."

Brontë turned her nose up.

"You're getting it muddy," said Shelley.

"Oh... Right," said Gretchen, picking them up again. She carried them to the trough and deposited them, feeling icy stares bore into her back. The heavy smell of alfalfa wafted up and made her want to sneeze as she undid the twine.

"So, uh... Anyone want to watch another movie with me tonight?"

"We don't have time tonight. We have to train," said Melville. "But maybe next week." He shook his nose at her. "But hey! Here's an idea... Why don't we show you how to plant next week, and then we can watch all the movies you have! We'll have a little party to celebrate you moving in." There was an odd edge to his voice. Gretchen felt her stomach sink. He knew.

"I won't be here next week. I'm not moving in. In fact, it's my cousin, Priscilla, who is moving in."

Hushed murmurs swept over the herd.

"So you're handing us off," Melville said. The betrayal in his tone caused Gretchen to shift her weight uncomfortably from foot to foot.

"Well... what did you expect?" she said, looking down to avoid the judgmental stare. "I'm not a farmer."

"Elsie was a great woman. She was kind and smart

and looked after us. Before she passed, she decided to leave this place to *you*. Not to Priscilla. Do you even care what happens to us?"

"I have to go study." Gretchen pushed past him in the direction of the house. A small *pft!* sound and a sudden wet feeling on her back caused her to stop short. "Did you just spit on me?"

The expression on Melville's face was one of such horror and embarrassment that Gretchen's own face turned a deep shade of pink in sympathy. He fled before she could say anything.

As she entered the house, Gretchen slid her soiled shirt over her head, careful to keep the glob of llama spit clear of her hair, and threw it into the washing machine. How dare Melville guilt trip her! He'd scarcely known her a day, and she didn't think she'd given him any reason to believe she would be staying. Surely it was obvious that she did not possess the level of responsibility required to maintain a place like this. The machine groaned to life and hummed as it started the cycle.

Shivering, Gretchen retreated to her room to find a new shirt. Her suitcase lay open on the floor, and she knelt to sort through the tangled mess of shirts and socks and underwear. A gray and green flannel came loose, and a few rolled-up pairs of socks tumbled out with it. Gretchen sniffled as she pulled it around her shoulders and stuck her arms through the sleeves. She sat there for a moment, tracing the grains in the floorboards. How had she managed to alienate a *llama?*

Neel watched her from his tank.

"Besides, vets work really long hours," Gretchen reasoned with him. "Priscilla will probably take much better care of Melville and the others than I can."

Neel didn't disagree.

"At least *you* understand."

The rest of the evening, Gretchen buried her nose in her books, but her glassy eyes ran over and over the walls of text without absorbing much information. The light from the windows faded, leaving the room feeling as empty and blue as she did. "But to keep it and stay here would be wrong. I'd screw it up," she told herself around the lump in her throat as she snapped the book shut. "And everyone would complain about that too."

Sleep welcomed Gretchen that night.

10: Bigger Neels

THE GREEN NUMBERS on the clock burned Gretchen's eyes and caused her to squint: 3:00 AM. A small groan escaped her and she shut her eyes again. The house was still quiet and dark, so in theory, it should've been easy to fall back to sleep, but tortured thoughts raced around her mind like greyhounds, preventing her from finding her way back into sweet oblivion. She was left with no choice but to get up.

The clock read 3:15 by the time Gretchen swung her legs over the edge of the bed and stretched. Maybe a walk would clear her mind. She pulled on a hoodie, her shoes, and a coat, picked up a flashlight, and headed out. The front door squealed as it swung shut behind her.

The world, still and quiet as the house, spread out around her, a vast and unknown landscape in the dark. It was an eerie feeling. Gretchen flicked the flashlight on. Its beam cut across the yard, biting back the darkness and bathing the damp earth and grasses in a pale yellow light.

Gretchen turned her steps toward the paddock, passing the barn where the llamas slept. Or at least, she *hoped* they were sleeping. She wouldn't know what to do if anyone witnessed them breaking into the lab again.

Wind whispered softly across the landscape, and Gretchen raised her eyes heavenward. The whole alien invasion story seemed far-fetched. But then again, so did talking llamas. The clouds still lingered overhead, higher and wispier than they'd been the day before, but if any flying saucers zoomed above them, she supposed she'd never know. Gretchen only caught glimpses of stars through patches in the cover.

She reached the edge of the property that faced the forest. Tall pines were silhouetted against the cloud cover, and for a moment, she considered continuing onward and exploring whatever mysteries were lying in the dark understory.

She sighed.

"I should probably go back now."

But her feet paid no heed to her words. She shivered and continued watching the shadows.

Suddenly, a light streaked down from the sky, and disappeared behind a stand of trees, followed by a loud, but low *BOOM*, which rattled the ground beneath Gretchen's feet. She staggered, and it took a moment for her to register what had happened. She straightened her glasses and stared at the spot where the light had disappeared.

"A meteorite!" she shouted, taking off running in the direction of the impact.

The horizon glowed as she reached the site, and as she passed the trees, the air became thick and dusty.

She slowed her pace.

Gretchen found herself gawking at the edge of a giant crater. "My gosh, the whole house could fit inside!" Kneeling, she squinted at its deepest point, about thirty feet down if she were to guess. "Ugh, what would that be, nine meters?" she mumbled, attempting to check the calculation in her head. Her gaze fell on a large lump at the bottom, but as the lump was a similar color to the earth, it was hard to make out exactly what it was in the grainy light of dawn. Probably the meteorite.

"Only one way to find out."

She carefully slid one leg over the edge. Dirt shimmered green wherever her shoe scraped against it. "That's probably the magnesium," she said to herself, stretching her arms to stay balanced against the sharp decline. "See? I can remember all of this when I don't need to. Why can't I remember it on test day?"

After nearly slipping a couple of times, she decided it would be better to crawl backwards on her hands and knees. Above, a glowing green trail clearly mapped out her footsteps. All her slips and bumped elbows, recorded. At last, the soles of her now-glowing shoes found the bottom. She stood, dusted herself off, and turned. Her breath caught and for a moment, she was unable to comprehend the thing that lay before her.

It wasn't a rock.

It was a creature.

Slowly pacing alongside its spine, she took in the spikes and the fading glow of the dust beneath it. The head tilted at an odd angle, resting slack-jawed on the ground, and its glassy eyes bulged. Gretchen ran her fingers over pointed teeth, which were each as long as her hand. A thin structure protruded from the fore-head, reminding her of the ornamentation on a female angler fish.

Whatever this thing was, it looked disturbingly similar to the Space Eel at the arcade, but that wasn't the most worrying part.

Heart beating in her throat, she took a few steps back from the lifeless body.

"A grown-up Neel."

GRETCHEN FOUND Melville waiting on her when she returned to the house.

"What are you doing?" he asked as she swooped

into the kitchen and set about pulling open every drawer and cabinet in the room. He seemed to have gotten over his embarrassment from the previous day, and had now returned to eying her as if she were the worst person in the world.

Gretchen ignored him.

"Aha!" she exclaimed as she found the knife drawer. The blades reflected the pale morning glow from the window. Gretchen gingerly felt the edges with her fingertips. Most were dull, so she had to settle for the least dull of the bunch. Melville approached and sniffed her.

"Your smell concerns me."

"Then stop smelling me," she said, wrapping each knife in a paper towel and packing them into her messenger bag. "It's weird."

She opened the cabinet under the sink and rummaged through dusty bottles of chemicals until she came up with a pair of rubber gloves. They were old and stiff, but they would have to do. For good measure, she grabbed a half-empty container of bleach as well. The label had long since faded and the ghost of the logo dated it by ten years. She winced as her hand closed around the grimy plastic. It, too, would have to do.

She got back to her feet and came face to face with Melville. His brown eyes held unrestrained judgment.

"What?" Gretchen demanded hotly.

"That's what I'm asking you. What do you think you're doing?" he said.

Gretchen resisted the urge to flick his nose. She didn't feel like getting spit on again. She adjusted the strap on her messenger bag and stood as tall as she could.

"I'm going to study biology. If you come along, you have to be quiet so I can focus."

She crossed the kitchen and let herself out through the garage door. To her surprise, Melville followed. She supposed his curiosity had gotten the better of him. As she passed the stacks of boxes, she stopped to grab a pair of old, rusty gardening shears. The llama eyed her curiously, but didn't say a word.

THE SUN HAD SLOWLY CREPT above the horizon while Gretchen wasn't looking. It took her a while to locate the crater again, but she finally recognized a stand of trees and found her bearings. She climbed over the lip of the crater and scrabbled her way to the bottom. The earth no longer glowed green when touched.

Melville's fuzzy ears appeared over the edge, but he didn't follow. He stared at the Eel carcass in horror.

"We have to burn this," he said.

Gretchen huffed as she sifted through her bag and pulled out a sketchbook. "You're such a spoilsport! This is a learning opportunity." She dug past her knives, a small makeup case, and a few plastic dinosaurs, and came up with a pencil. Though the eraser was chewed to almost nothing, the graphite was intact. She offered a cheeky smile to Melville. "Plus, who else in the history of ever has gotten an up-close look at eel guts... Space Alien Eel guts? I could write a book and be famous!"

He didn't look amused. "Elsie did."

Gretchen ignored him and to her surprise, he made no move to stop her.

The first order of business was to inspect the external features. She paced around the body once more, but this time, she grasped the pencil and the sketchbook in her hands. She'd never considered herself much of a serious artist, but with a bit of work, she managed to capture a sufficient likeness of the Eel on paper: the dorsal spikes, the odd colorless spots that ran along the lateral line, the many, many, many teeth... She made sure to snap pictures at various angles with her phone camera as well.

Taking note of the creature's swollen middle, she tucked the sketchbook beneath her armpit and clambered up onto its side. Dead flesh squished beneath her shoes, sending a shudder through her body, but she quickly shook off the squeamishness. She knelt and placed a hand against its skin. It felt like silk as she ran her hand toward the tail, but prickled her palm as she pulled it back in the opposite direction.

Skin like a shark's, she jotted in the sketchbook.

The spots turned out to be regularly spaced diamond-shaped patches of pale discoloration. Gretchen assumed that, like the bulb on its head—the anterior ornamentation—they were probably once phosphorescent. She made more sketches and notes, and took more photos before hopping to the ground once more.

Then, placing the book in the relative safety of her messenger bag, she withdrew a bag of markers, the gardening shears, and the knives.

Her brow furrowed as she studied the Eel, and she took a deep breath.

The second order of business: plan out the incisions.

Gretchen uncapped a permanent marker and approached the Eel carcass. Its width matched her height, so she had to stoop a little to draw a line from its throat, down its middle, and all the way to the cloaca. The belly was tight and bloated, making it easier to draw on, and the marker tip glided over the smooth skin. Gretchen braced her wrist to keep the line steady.

Once satisfied with her work, she donned the rubber gloves, then took up one of the sharper knives and poked it into the throat. She made a slit across, and then, exchanging her knife for the shears, began cutting lengthwise through the skin. Periodically, she stopped to make a vertical slit in the body for ease of prying it open.

Muddy-colored blood oozed in viscous clumps wherever she cut, and soon the shears became too gummed-up to use. Tossing the tool aside, she peeled back several layers of epidermis to reveal the striated muscle beneath.

"Okay, it looks like a normal fish so far," Gretchen panted, tugging at the fingers of her gloves. The cool air brought relief to her sweaty palms. She sketched the muscles, paying attention to where they connected and how they might move. When she finished, she pulled the gloves back on and continued to work.

Soon, the muscles of the first half of the body were cut and splayed open to reveal the body cavity. To Gretchen's disappointment, they followed the pattern of a normal vertebrate organ system. However, she did find what looked to be large, elongated air sacs that ran the length of the creature. *That must've been what kept it afloat*, she thought. But she couldn't work out how the Eel became airborne in the first place. The heart had four chambers. She paused to take note of this, along with the air sacs.

When Gretchen moved on to the digestive system, she noticed that the stomach appeared painfully distended and lumpy. She jammed her knife into the organ and, grunting with effort, sawed it open. Putrid green goo poured forth in a heavy stream, drenching her gloves, splattering tiny droplets onto her skin, and causing her to gag and cough. The sickly-sweet smell burned her nostrils and the back of her throat, but somehow, she managed to peel back the stomach lining. A cow head flopped out and she shrieked. The thing hung limply from the neck it was attached to. Its bulky body remained lodged inside the digestive cavity.

"This is probably what killed you!" she sputtered through tears. She felt the sore urge to rub her stinging eyes, but didn't dare bring her reeking hands anywhere near her face.

From the ridge of the crater, Melville pretended not to watch. "Are you done yet?" he called in a bored tone.

"You sure you don't want to come see this?"

"I'm sure."

Gretchen shrugged and resumed cutting down the belly, toward the tail. It wasn't long before she reached another swollen organ. She cut into it without a problem, but nearly dropped her knife in surprise as she opened it.

Eggs. Hundreds of gelatinous, softball-sized eggs, crammed inside the body cavity. Gretchen reached out to touch one, recalling the slick, watery feeling of Neel's egg. Yep. These were just as slimy. However, she could clearly see that the embryos weren't fully formed yet. Neel's egg had been in a ditch. This Eel must've been hanging around, waiting to deposit her clutch in the nearest puddle of water.

Gretchen continued to work, and as soon as she was satisfied that she'd conducted a thorough investigation, she took a step back. It was only then that she noticed she'd been holding her breath. Her lungs ached for a proper breath of air. She backpedaled a few more feet, and only then did she dare to breathe in. Gretchen sucked in gulps of air, but instantly regretted it as her mouth became filled with the stench of Eel guts, which emanated off her in waves. "Want to burn it now?" she said between coughs. "It's too big to pickle."

Melville's ears tilted smugly at her. "I have a better idea. Let's come back here tonight."

Gretchen tried to shake some of the fluids off her arms, but only succeeded in getting flecks on her glasses. "A bonfire? Suit yourself. I'm not roasting marshmallows over that thing."

Melville laughed.

As they neared the farmhouse, Billy's truck, with Gretchen's car in tow, pulled into the driveway. Gravel crackled beneath the tires and the vehicle groaned as the old farmer slowed his truck to a crawling speed beside Gretchen and Melville. He leaned out the window with a grin.

"I called the house several times, and figured you was busy with farm work." His nose crinkled and he waved a hand in front of it. "Seems I was right! What in the world did you get yourself into?"

Gretchen cast an anxious glance at Melville, who pretended to stare into the distance in a llama-like fashion. She ran a hand through her hair, and immediately regretted it as a streak of sticky goo met her scalp. Her lips curled in disgust.

"UGH! NO!"

Billy wheezed with laughter. "Go on and get cleaned up! I'll leave your car in the driveway."

He pulled the rest of the way up to the house.

Melville turned to Gretchen. "You really should do something about the smell."

Rolling her eyes, she followed the truck.

Gretchen headed straight for the shower the moment she stepped into the farmhouse. She peeled away her disgusting clothes and hurled them into the washer, then locked herself in the bathroom and ran the shower water as hot as she could without scalding herself. The streams of clean water brought sweet relief. Gretchen scrubbed at her skin until it burned red and the awful feeling of the Eel innards fell away and spiraled down the drain.

11: Elvers

Night fell, and Melville appeared at the front door to meet Gretchen. "Leave that here," he said when he spied the large flashlight in her hand.

"Are you sure?" Gretchen said. Her skin prickled as she caught the green glow flashing in his eyes as he moved his head. Llamas weren't supposed to see in the dark. At the right angle, cats, dogs, and spiders all had that reflective glow caused by a thin membrane at the back of the eye. Not llamas. She gave a nervous laugh and wiggled the frames of her glasses. "I don't see so well. Even worse at night."

"You won't need it for what we're looking at tonight," he insisted.

Gretchen reluctantly set the flashlight by the umbrella stand, stepped out of the house, and shut the door, extinguishing the light. Melville's hooves knocked against the porch and pebbles scraped against each other as he stepped to the gravel path. Gretchen took a breath, blinking until her eyes adjusted as much as they could to the low light levels, then followed him. He set a brisk pace, and she had to jog to keep up.

"So... If we're not burning the Eel, what are we doing with it?"

"Letting the others dispose of it."

She slowed to a halt. Frogs could be heard calling in the distance. Their *peeps* and *criiiiiicks* defied the chill air, heralding the onset of spring. It all seemed so normal.

"Others?" she repeated.

"Others."

For the first time in a very long time, Gretchen gazed up at the vast, sparkling sky. And for the first time ever, she felt at a loss as to exactly what was out there. She used to think she knew it all. Like many girls, she'd gone through a space phase when she was small, and had spent hours poring over every astronomy book she could find at the library, learning the names of the planets and the stories intertwined with the stars. But eventually, she'd moved on. Now, with a little effort, she picked out the Big Dipper and Orion's Belt. She was pleased to find that the knowledge was still there, even if a bit rusty. She eagerly searched around for the North Star. That had been her favorite.

Melville butted his head against her back. "Come along. We don't want to miss it."

The ground was still slick, and Gretchen stumbled along behind him, occasionally reaching out to place a hand on his woolly side so she wouldn't fall.

"Tell me again why we left the flashlight," she grunted as she pulled her foot out of a hole.

"So we can actually see them," the llama said with an impatient swish of his tail as he waited for her to finish shaking the mud off her shoe. "This is a once in a lifetime event. Evidence shows that these things only breed once every fifty years, and they always return to the exact spot where they were hatched."

"This farm."

Melville nodded.

"Is that what they're doing here now? Breeding?"

"You cut an awful lot of eggs out of the dead one this morning. And that monster you insist on keeping only hatched a few days ago. I daresay we'll have luck with finding what I'm expecting to find tonight."

"Is this the reason you and the herd broke into the lab the other night?"

"They've been picking up hints of Eels for weeks now."

They came to the edge of the crater and Gretchen started to swing her leg over to descend. Melville caught her shirt in his teeth and pulled her back.

"It's safer to stay here."

She squinted into the darkness, trying to make out the shape of the Eel carcass. Its stench hung heavy in the air. A breeze sifted by and she nearly gagged.

"Shh!" Melville hissed. "They're here."

At first, Gretchen thought they were fireflies. Pale, drifting lights, blinking fuzzily in the night. But it was too early and far too cold for fireflies. As they drew closer, she saw that they weren't insects at all, but tiny Eels.

They illuminated the night with a soft yellow hue. In size and shape, they appeared to be a bit older than Neel—if put in regular eel terms, the elver stage, which succeeded the glass eel stage.

Gretchen gasped as she watched them drift. "They're so cute!"

The elvers twined through the air like ribbons in the wind, emitting high-pitched squeals as they drew closer to the body.

"Just watch," Melville said. "You won't call them 'cute' in a minute."

The squeals turned into shrieks as the small creatures nuzzled up to the carcass, where they began to rip and tear at the dead flesh. Razor teeth glinted and flashed as they snipped and snapped. Soon, the entirety of the area was covered in a wriggling mass of feeding elvers. Bits and pieces of their feast flew in the frenzy, and those on the outskirts chased down the scraps and devoured them, mid-air, like ravenous wolves.

It was over in minutes. There wasn't a trace left—not even the skeleton. Gretchen stared in horror as the throng disbanded and dispersed, stomachs now bulging with their meal.

"And they don't only eat dead things," said Melville. "Do you really want to let your cousin turn this place into a tourist destination?"

THEY HEADED BACK to the farmhouse at a brisk pace. Gretchen's head spun. She teetered back and forth between amazement and wanting to scream. Her heart pounded at the thought of giant Eels, flying above the farm, but the significance of their existence wasn't lost on her. How could no one know about this? That thing must've been fifty feet long! The cheap cardboard cutouts in the arcade burned in her mind's eye. Maybe someone already did.

She typed out a text to Harley and slid the phone back into her pocket. He probably wouldn't answer until tomorrow afternoon.

When they reached the llama paddock, she found the herd strewn about the yard, moping.

"Look, everyone. I'm sorry," she announced without preamble. "I shouldn't have told Priscilla I was selling the farm before consulting you. This has been your home longer than mine, and you deserved a say."

Brontë turned her nose up with a *hmph!*

Beside her, Verne spit into the grass.

"Can we please talk this out?" Gretchen tried.

"I don't think so," Shelley said.

Melville marched to the front of the group, and Austen and Twain let out bleats of protest as he bumped into them. He stood by Gretchen's elbow and addressed the herd in a commanding tone. "Stop sulking and come inside."

The other llamas raised their heads, ears tilted toward him.

"We have a Code 243."

Eyes widened, revealing their whites. Everyone got to their hooves and followed Melville into the house, expressions suddenly grim. Gretchen would've been hurt by their cold demeanors toward her, had not the sense of urgency been almost palpable. They filed through the front door and into the living room, where they gathered into a circle and directed their attention at Melville.

"They've begun feeding," he announced.

Shelley swore softly. "How much time do we have?"

Melville glanced at the sky out the window. "Maybe a few days."

Gretchen followed his line of sight. Silver stars

pricked the blackened sky, and at the edge of her vision, she could've sworn she saw a few move. But when she tried to pinpoint the movement, she lost sight of it.

"We need to begin extermination now, before it gets out of hand," said Austen.

"Yes," agreed Einstein. "Once they infect this farm, they'll devastate everything and then spread like a disease. It will become an impossible war."

"We should start with that *thing* living in Elsie's room," said Brontë.

Gretchen blinked, tearing her attention from the window. "Neel?"

"Yes, that one must've escaped our notice when we stamped out the eggs in that ditch," said Melville.

"You did what?" asked Gretchen.

Melville turned to her. "A few days before you arrived, we found an egg mass in that ditch. It alerted us that the Eels were beginning to arrive and we did our best to eliminate them. From what you just saw, we missed quite a few. But no matter. We'll take care of the problem."

She startled as the group moved in the direction of the bedroom. "Wait," she said, following them. But they ignored her and continued down the hall. Gretchen pushed her way through the llamas to get to the door. She slammed it shut and turned to face the herd with an angry glare. "Hang on! You're not harming my pet!"

Melville frowned. "Your 'pet' will become a monster. It will eat anything and everything and decimate this farm before moving on and doing the same to the next. You saw what happened at the carcass. It will become a plague, a blight on this earth."

Gretchen tightened her grip on the doorknob and steeled her tone. "Neel won't hurt anything. I'm training him."

Melville's own tone was stony. "His kind cannot be trained. They are bottomless pits and killing machines."

She opened her mouth to protest, but he cut her off with a shake of his head. "You're a scientist, so think about it logically. Yes, Neel is manageable now. He fits in a tank and you feed him table scraps." He paused, as if waiting for Gretchen to agree, but she refused to acknowledge anything he was about to say. He flicked his ears and pressed on with his argument. "But he will outgrow that tank and your table scraps. What happens when he gets to be an adult? What happens when his appetite continues to grow? Either you really want to take care of this place—of us—or you don't. You have to decide."

Though Gretchen shook her head, the truth of his words sank in. Neel was small now, but he would probably reach the elver stage in a matter of days.

Then what? She could find a bigger tank, but how long would it be before he outgrew that? And what would she feed him? What if he escaped? She recalled how he snapped at her fingers and shuddered. If he was that willing to bite the hand that fed him, what would happen when the hand plus the rest of the body could be swallowed in a single gulp?

Gretchen drew in a pained breath, feeling her grip on the doorknob relax. She barely saw her shoes, despite the fact she stared right at them. "Okay. But we're doing this humanely."

The llamas stepped back and allowed her to pass by as she headed for the kitchen. She found a bottle of alcohol and a knife, which she carried into the bathroom. By the time she fetched the aquarium from the bedroom, she felt as if she were walking in a haze.

A stream of water splashed into the bathtub as she tilted the heavy glass tank. It splattered loudly against the enamel, but she could barely hear it above her pounding heart. Neel swam against the current with frantic undulations. He looked so frightened that Gretchen pulled the tank up sharply, stopping the flow. She turned to the others, panting.

"I can't do this."

Melville stepped forward. His usual no-nonsense expression became gentle. "We can take care of it if you would like to step out."

Gretchen shook as she wrapped her arms around

the tank. "No! He's mine! I rescued him and I'm not going to let you hurt him!" She reached into the water and ran a finger along the Eel's silky body. "I won't let him become a monster."

"Gretchen. There's only one way you can keep that promise."

But she ignored him and reached to turn the faucet on. When it warmed, she picked up a nearby bucket and filled it to the brim. The water conditioner sat on the rim of the bathtub, where she'd left it. She picked it up, but when she tried to read the recommended amounts, her eyes blurred.

"I can figure this out. I know I'm not the smartest or most qualified, but I swear—I won't rest until he's trained."

The llamas watched as she mopped her tears with the hem of her shirt before guestimating the amount of conditioner needed. Several drops into the bucket would presumably neutralize any bad chemicals. Gretchen poured in a few more, then gave it a minute before hefting the bucket up to the rim of the aquarium. With wobbly arms, she tilted the bucket forward, sloshing its contents into Neel's tank. Neel, unhappy with all the disturbances, wriggled against the glass again.

The water settled out, as did Neel's urgency, and he resumed his silent, watchful manner. Gretchen's now-pruney fingers stroked his side. This time, he didn't turn or snap. Behind her, the llamas whispered amongst themselves. Their low voices sounded argumentative and urgent. After a moment, Melville and Einstein stepped forward. Melville cleared his throat.

"Though we wholeheartedly believe it best to eliminate the Eels before they become a threat, we realize that the farm now belongs to you. Our greatest wish is to honor Elsie's wishes, and she must've had a good reason for entrusting us to you."

Gretchen ran the back of her wrist over her nose and squared her shoulders. "This happened before. There have to be answers, either in this house or in the lab. Give me the rest of the night to think, and we'll reconvene in the morning and make a plan. Sound good?"

She received a few halfhearted murmurs of agreement.

"We will see you in the morning," said Melville. "We're looking forward to your big solution."

With that, the llamas retreated, their hooves thumping against the floorboards until they exited the house.

12: Quick Study

THE TENSION in Gretchen's muscles didn't subside until the herd left the bathroom. She sat on the side of the tub, stroking Neel until she stopped trembling. Then, with a small groan, she stood with the aquarium and returned to her room. She set Neel on his stand and then closed the bedroom door.

"My, we've gotten ourselves into a pickle, haven't we?" she said, leaning back against the door.

Neel watched her. She wasn't sure if she imagined the betrayal in his eyes or not.

"I'm sorry," she sighed. "I don't know how to deal with panicked llamas or alien invasions. But I'm *not* going to let anything happen to you, okay?"

He said nothing.

She tried to imagine what he would be like when he reached his next developmental stage and was suddenly filled with visions of him tearing the flesh from her body while she slept.

"We're all going to die, aren't we?"

Neel swam in a circle, bumping his nose against the glass. Gretchen put her head in her hands.

"I should've told Penelope 'no' during our first phone call. I should've said I have to study." She let out a chuckle and rubbed her temples. "It would've been a lie, but it would've kept me out of this mess."

She turned to Neel again. "Did you know that I don't even want to be a vet anymore? I haven't told anyone that, but I've known that for a long time now. I don't know what to do—I already told everyone I would take the test and get into the vet program. I'm burnt out and I can hardly bring myself to look at my textbooks anymore!" She ran a hand through her hair. "But I guess it doesn't matter because your cousins are probably going to eat me. Problem solved, I guess..."

The Eel nibbled at his tail. Gretchen paced.

"Elsie seemed to think you were worth keeping around. From what I've seen so far, she dedicated her life to it."

She came to a halt by the bed.

"She left her house to me. Her house and all her research. I don't know why, but I think she thought I could finish it." She drew in a deep breath and pushed all thoughts of school and stress from her mind. She knew how to research. She knew how to dig up information. "I can be a quick study when I want to be," she said firmly to herself. Sinking to her knees, she peered underneath the bed. The file folder she'd picked up at the lab had been kicked beneath it. Neel watched as she opened it and ran her eyes over the documents. "Thank you, Elsie," she whispered. "Sorry Neel, but Eels don't run this farm. I do."

The night wore on and Gretchen poured over the file. Its contents shocked her, but no more so than any of the other events that had transpired the past two days. When she finished reading, she headed to the living room and began methodically picking through each and every one of Elsie's notebooks, sorting the useful ones into a stack at her feet.

One passage in particular caused her to drop the book and run to the garage. Dust flew as she pulled the lid off the first box she came to and tossed it to the side. She sifted through the faded notes until she found what she was looking for. "What the heck," she breathed. Replacing the lid, she carried the box back to the living room, where she resumed pouring over the journals.

At last, in the early hours of the morning, Gretchen fell asleep on the couch, an open journal balanced on her stomach.

13: Information

"You have telekinesis!" Gretchen exclaimed.

Einstein flinched back from the finger being jabbed at his nose. His ears flattened. "I beg your pardon?"

The llamas had woken Gretchen around mid-morning. She'd refused to speak to them until she'd checked on Neel and gotten something to eat. Now, they were all gathered around the dining room table where she had spread out all the documents, journals, and several boxes from the garage. Exhaustion caused her to sway where she stood, but she firmly crossed her arms and frowned at the bespectacled llama.

"Why have you been hiding it?"

Melville shoved Gretchen's arm away with his snout. "Don't harass him."

Her face fell. "You seriously don't know? But your file says—"

"His file?" interrupted Austen. Hushed murmurs broke out among them.

"Yes, his file. You all have one," Gretchen said, pointing to seven stacks of papers at one end of the table. "You weren't abducted by aliens. You were a part of a training program to fight the Eels. How can you not remember this?"

Einstein bent over the documents and read a few lines before pulling back. "Gretchen, I don't *want* to remember this. I don't think any of us do."

She blinked. "Why?"

The others pawed nervously at the floor with ears flat against their heads. Uneasy hums filled the room.

"Why did you have to bring this up?" demanded Melville.

"Because the scientists who raised you equipped you to be able to handle the Eels. They really wanted you to keep them in check and they cared about you too. They—"

But Melville stopped her. "Our time with the aliens was horrible and cruel. We wanted to forget."

Gretchen's hands moved to her hips. "Would you rather be eaten by Eels?" When no one answered, she sighed. "Let's move on and we'll circle back to this." She picked up a faded and yellowed piece of paper. "Elsie and her husband had a plan in place to contain the invasion. I think we should give it a shot."

Clearing her throat, she read the note aloud:

My Dear Elsie—

The shrink ray is working beautifully. I've found that the material we collected on our last excursion is a much more effective source of power than electricity. I am going out to pick up a few more supplies and should be home in time for dinner.

With love,
Owlen

Gretchen slapped a hand against the surface of the table. The words didn't quite have the effect she had hoped for, and she was met with confused expressions. "He and Elsie wanted to shrink the Eels!" she pressed.

"That's crazy," said Shelley.

Ducking her head, Gretchen sifted through the papers and came up with what looked like blueprints for a very large laser. "Any crazier than talking llamas or Space Eels?"

She turned the paper so the others could see. "Will you help me?"

Einstein stepped forward and squinted at the designs. After a long moment, he met Gretchen's eyes. "Anything you want us to do, we can figure it out and talk you through it," he said. He flicked his ears at her hands. "But whatever it is you're thinking, you'll have to be the one to actually do it because... you have thumbs."

"I want to build this shrink ray," she said. "I want a bunch of little Neels."

Einstein blinked. "I'm not sure how that would fix the problem."

"We can try!" Melville cut in. "We'll go through the plans and figure out how to build this." His voice became hard. "And if it doesn't work, we'll do it our way."

Gretchen nodded solemnly. She opened up the lid of one of the boxes. Then another. Then another, uncovering various tools and pieces of equipment. "I think these are the pieces for the laser. We probably have everything we need to build it in this house."

"What about the power source Owlen mentioned?" asked Einstein.

"I have a hunch." She picked up one of the journals and flipped through the pages again.

Drawings of faraway places, creatures, and people flew past her vision, but at last, she came to a page with a diagram similar to the one she'd made earlier. Elsie's drawings held a refinement to them that Gretchen's lacked, and she easily recognized the various organs she'd sifted through. A phantom stench tickled at her nostrils as she traced her finger along the notes on the digestive tract.

Another page detailed their life history. Gretchen recognized drawings similar to what Neel's egg had looked like, and others that looked like newly hatched Neel. The next stages showed the development of spikes and ornamentation. It was a strange feeling, seeing it all compiled like this.

Finally, she came to the page she sought. It read like a correspondence.

Dear Reader,

The creatures follow a loose hierarchy based solely on size. The larger individuals will have their fill of a kill. Whenever possible, they swallow it whole. If not, any remains are left to the young or weak. I assume—as with many reptiles and amphibians—they engage in cannibalism, but I have yet to observe it. This may explain the hesitation of the smaller individuals. Social interaction between conspecifics seems virtually nonexistent.

Or so I thought...

Yesterday, I had the thrilling opportunity to observe an interaction between the Queen and several of her subordinates in the vicinity. I was observing some of the subadults when she drifted into view over the barley field on the west side of the property. Immediately, they halted their hunting and their attention riveted on her. The Queen slowed her flight and began to bioluminesce in complicated patterns. Much to my surprise, the subadults did not hide, but copied her patterns. It was one of the most hypnotic phenomena I have ever witnessed. I want to study it further.

Of course, the others are still bent on eliminating the creatures. I don't blame them, but I can't help but wonder if there may be a way to coexist. It would be a shame to lose a species we have only begun to know, and who knows what its destruction may do to the balance of things. Owlen is working on a solution. I laughed when he first mentioned it to me, but he was in earnest. For my part, I will continue to observe and record. I pray we find a solution soon.

−Elsie Hildegard

The illustration beside the letter sent chills

through Gretchen's blood. A massive Eel loomed over a collection of elvers and smaller adults. Frills and other ornamentation surrounded its face, flared out in some sort of display. Beside the lure on her head, Elsie had written: *Boosts the signal.*

Gretchen turned the journal toward the llamas, who took a few steps back in fright. "This is what we're up against." She held out the blueprints in her other hand. "And this is how we're going to do it."

A visible shiver ran through the herd, except for Einstein, who leaned over the blueprints, squinting. "Yes, I think I can talk you through this," he said.

"Great!" said Gretchen.

"I still don't understand why we're not just going to take them out," said Shelley.

"It doesn't matter," said Melville. "Gretchen knows what she's doing. She won't let us down."

Gretchen wasn't sure she liked the edge in his tone, but she ignored it as she thought. They would build the laser, and then what? She needed to find a way to power it. She had a good idea of where the power source might have disappeared, but... no. *No.* It was too far-fetched. Her phone buzzed, interrupting her frantic circles. Harley. She opened the message.

HARLEY

Why do you need to know who built the arcade?

Heart pounding in her ears, she tapped Harley's contact information, hit the call symbol, and put the phone to her ear. It rang for a full minute before he picked up.

"Why are you calling? You don't usually call."

"I need to use the arcade."

"You know I don't care if you come in." The phone rustled as if he were moving it from his shoulder. "This round's sold out! Come back in fifteen minutes!"

Gretchen waited patiently for him to move the phone back and turn his attention on her again. "No, I mean, I need to use the arcade tonight, after it closes."

"After midnight? Why the hell do you want to play laser tag that late?"

Gretchen shifted from foot to foot. "Because... I need to practice. And my friends need to practice. And... My friends wouldn't be allowed in under normal circumstances."

There was a long pause. "Who are they? Escaped convicts? Politicians?"

"No! Nothing like that! Just... Can you open it? For me?"

"I don't like this."

"What if I told you that the fate of the world depended on it?"

Harley chuckled. "So they're conspiracy theorists."

"Harley!" Gretchen said. "Focus! Can you open the arcade for me? This is important."

Silence filled the small pause. She held her breath, readying another argument in case she needed it. But she didn't. Her friend let out a groan. "You're going to get me fired."

A smile spread over Gretchen's face. "Thanks! You're the best! One more thing..."

"What?" He sounded disgruntled.

"I need the lava lamp."

"Gretchen!"

"Again. The world. The entire world hinges on you letting me borrow a stupid prop. I'll bring it back."

He groaned. "Yep. I'll start looking at job postings."

"Thanks!" She hung up and faced the herd. "I know a place where we can do a practice run of the invasion."

"What are you talking about?" Shelley asked, rolling her eyes. "We can't practice without the Eels, unless you're planning on letting us use your demon pet as a target."

"No one is touching Neel. Did Elsie own a truck trailer?"

"Yeah. It's in the barn," said Twain.

"Help me get it out."

14: Jury-Rigged

With the herd's assistance, Gretchen coaxed an old truck trailer out of the barn. Its wheels resisted valiantly, but with an ear-splitting groan, the stubborn things were convinced into rolling. The group spent half an hour cleaning it of rust and spiders— Gretchen, with her towels, and the llamas, with their fluffy tails. Melville, nose to an old manual, talked Gretchen through attaching the trailer hitch to her car, and then how to hook up the trailer. However, the trailer's frame was awfully heavy, and Gretchen and Melville fell to arguing about whether or not it was properly attached.

In the end, they decided to call Billy. Or rather, Gretchen did. When he arrived, they stood outside the barn, examining the trailer and Gretchen's car. Billy looked baffled as he stared at it. The llamas watched him with concern.

"So you want to attach this," he indicated the trailer, "to this," he indicated the car.

"Yes," Gretchen said.

The wrinkles on his forehead scrunched. "Why?"

"I need to take one of the llamas to the vet," she lied. Melville snorted at her unconvincing tone. "It will be a quick trip."

"Very quick if we all die," muttered Shelley. Twain frantically bopped her neck with his nose, but Billy scratched his head, as if he hadn't heard.

"Can it be done?" Gretchen asked.

"It can... Might tear your car up more if you try hauling anything too heavy."

She smiled. "Perfect! I pulled Elsie's tools out. Let me know how I can help."

AFTER ATTACHING THE TRAILER HITCH, it didn't take Billy long to hook the trailer to the car, but he spent half an hour more checking that the connection would hold. Gretchen hovered, carefully watching what he did in case she needed to reattach anything.

"They look like they belong to each other," she said with a wince as they stepped back to admire his handiwork. Her dented car and the dingy trailer— she doubted they would get very far once on the road.

"This really isn't the safest thing," Billy said. "I

wouldn't advise going very far with it. Definitely don't drive it on the highway."

"Okay. Thanks for your help," said Gretchen as she saw him back to his truck. She waited until he'd pulled off the property before addressing the herd.

"Who's ready for a road trip?"

The llamas all exchanged glances.

"He said it wasn't safe to drive," said Austen.

"It won't be safe to stay here and watch Eels overrun the place, either," said Gretchen. "We need to do something."

Melville stepped forward. "We're willing to do whatever it takes to stop them, even if it means riding in a broken-down trailer pulled by your broken-down car."

The others nodded.

Einstein stepped forward. "I think I should stay here and read about the laser," he said. "I can also keep an eye on the radar."

Gretchen nodded. "Will you be okay by yourself?"

He swallowed. "I can do this."

Gretchen led him into the house and had him watch as she scrawled her cell phone number on a piece of paper. She taped it to the wall, next to Elsie's phone. She was glad the numbers were big. "Call me if you need anything," she said.

After running through how to operate the phone

several times, Gretchen kissed him on the top of his nose. "Hold the fort down, here. We'll be back soon."

15: Closing Doors

THE LLAMAS STEPPED into the trailer with cautious hooves. It rattled and groaned under their weight, but held firm. All of Gretchen's mother's concerns over her decrepit vehicle came flooding back into her mind as she watched it bounce and shudder when Verne boarded.

"You're going to kill us all," grumbled Shelley.

Gretchen gave what she considered a convincing laugh, though whether she was trying to convince herself or the llamas, she wasn't sure. "No I'm not," she said, picking up a large wooden board and sliding it into the front of the trailer in hopes that it would help block some of the wind. "I'll drive slow, just don't jump out."

She made sure they had enough space as she set up boards to provide as much shelter from the wind as possible. Once satisfied, she went back to the house to pack an overnight bag, and after a bit of thought, dug through the garage until she came up with a large bucket with a lid. She transferred Neel into it, only filling the water partway, then poked a few holes in the lid and snapped it on. Einstein probably wouldn't do anything against her wishes, but she felt it best to keep a watchful eye over the little Eel.

At last, Gretchen stashed Neel on the passenger side floorboard and climbed into the driver's seat. She figured she must've been shaking more than the car as she started the engine. The water in Neel's bucket sloshed disconcertingly as soon as she took her foot off the brake, and she quickly pressed it again, causing the water to slosh even more.

"I'm so sorry, Neel!" she cried, and then gave a stressed squeal.

"Everything alright?" called Melville.

"Absolutely!" she answered.

This was going to be a long drive.

The car groaned and lurched as she started down the driveway and the water in the bucket splashed wildly, but she made it to the road without any mishap. She leaned out her window. From her vantage point, she couldn't see the llamas, and assumed they were huddled on the floor of the trailer. Returning to her seat, she drew in a deep breath and continued on.

Pieces of azure sky peeked from between puffy clouds, and stretches of fields and woods rolled by. Gretchen found that playing music lessened the sound of the sloshing water, thereby lessening her anxiety. She didn't have any trouble until she reached the on-ramp for the highway. Ever so gently, she pressed the brake, but the momentum of the whole ridiculous contraption still jolted her forward a couple more inches past the yield sign than she'd wanted to be.

The on-ramp sloped steeply downward until it joined up with the highway below. Her hands trembled as she adjusted her white-knuckled grip on the steering wheel and peered down at it, trying to determine the best way of tackling the situation. A loud *SPLAT!* startled her, and the car lurched forward another few inches. She turned in her seat to find a big glob of spit decorating the rear windshield. Leaning out the driver's side window, she shot a glare at Melville. He wiggled his ears apologetically.

"What?" Gretchen said. The seatbelt dug into her chest and shoulder as she propped her elbow against the car door.

"We were wondering if everything was alright," he said. "We haven't moved in a few minutes."

"Everything is fine. I'm waiting for an opening."

Shelley's head turned as a single car drove past, but the llama said nothing. Gretchen settled herself in the seat again, grumbling. Once sure that the way forward was clear, she carefully let her foot off the brake.

Roller coasters had nothing on the ride that followed. At first, nothing happened. But as Gretchen feathered the gas pedal, they began to move. Slowly, slowly. But as the contraption fully entered the ramp, the weight shifted and the car picked up speed, barreling toward the merging lane. She let out a shriek as she bumped onto the road. A horn blared out of nowhere, and a car sped past in the neighboring lane. The sound changed in pitch and faded as the other car became a speck in the distance.

"The Doppler Effect," she murmured weakly.

She earned a few more honks as she set a slow pace, frequently glancing back to make sure the herd was okay. But as she got the hang of driving the unwieldy thing, she grew more comfortable and relaxed. She glanced at her side mirror and smirked. Six llama heads stuck above the makeshift wind barrier, their noses twitching as they reveled in the ride.

"What about that, Neel?"

Neel didn't respond.

They reached the city early in the evening. Gretchen found a rest stop to pull into and collect herself before heading into the more crowded city streets. The llamas stumbled from the trailer on wobbly legs. When they realized that no one had remembered to pack dinner, they wandered over to a sad patch of grass behind the rest area and nibbled at the pitiful blades.

Gretchen paced for a bit, then settled at a picnic table. She stuck her fingers through the mesh of the tabletop, nervously picking at the metal grating. Melville approached her.

"Are we almost there?" he asked.

"Yeah. I need to make a stop by the veterinary clinic and let my boss know I need a few more days off," she said. "She's not going to be happy."

Melville was quiet for a moment. "Why do you want to be a veterinarian so bad?" he asked.

Gretchen shrugged. After the long drive, she didn't have the energy to pretend to be excited about her career choices.

"There must be some reason?"

"I like helping animals. And everyone said I would be good at it. And…" she paused. "Well… I said I was going to do it. I've been saying I want to be a vet since high school. I took all the classes, read all the books, volunteered at the shelters—I can't go back now! All my teachers and professors kept saying I was on track, and I wasn't going to have any trouble getting into vet school. But I can't. And I feel like I'm disappointing everyone." She propped her elbows on the table.

"Those are all terrible reasons," said Melville.

"Yep."

"What's going to happen after the Eels?" Melville asked.

"You mean if we're not eaten?" Gretchen said with a small laugh.

"No, I'm serious. Are you going to come back here, to the city?"

To Gretchen's surprise, there wasn't any trace of judgment in his tone. She sat back and closed her eyes, picturing what it would be like to live permanently at Hildegard Farm. The property was so pretty, and come April, it would be even prettier. The thought of going back to her cramped, dirty apartment made her grimace until she was sure her face resembled Priscilla's. When she opened her eyes, she found Melville watching her carefully.

"My lease doesn't end for six more months, so I have to," she said lamely.

He nodded.

Thoughts of farm life played out in Gretchen's mind the entire way to the clinic. It would be hard, and there would be a lot of downsides. Long hours, sore muscles, brutal summers, and a dependence on plants actually growing. That part caused her stomach to knot.

But... Elsie apparently trusted her. She didn't know why, but she'd trusted her. And she had to admit, some parts seemed appealing. No more testing. No more trying to impress professors or bosses. She could search for amphiumas any time she wanted. She could learn to plant and harvest. The thought of the llamas teaching her their farming process made her lips twitch into a faint smile. She could see herself learning from them.

They reached the veterinary clinic twenty minutes before closing. Gretchen left the car running. She didn't bank on her errand taking long and didn't want to risk the engine giving out after a rest. Heads raised as Gretchen pulled open the door to the little building.

Her boss looked up from where she stood at the front counter. "I thought you weren't getting back until tomorrow?" she said, her brow furrowing.

Gretchen nodded. "I know. I hate to do this to you, but I need to quit, effective immediately."

The words tumbled out as if on their own accord. Gretchen was so stunned at what she'd said that she forgot to close her mouth, as if she expected her words to crawl back inside. But there was no taking them back.

"Be sure to clean out your drawer. It's a bit of a mess," her boss said before returning to typing at the computer.

Gretchen blinked.

No resistance.

No disappointment.

"Oh." She walked over to her desk and pulled open the drawer, feeling as if the entire world was watching her. But when she threw a glance over her shoulder, everyone continued to be absorbed in whatever they were doing before she'd barged in. She took the drawer completely out of the desk, and dumped the pencils, doodles, and animal-shaped erasers into her messenger bag. Replacing the drawer, she took one last look around the clinic.

It felt too easy. She'd been working here a whole year, and now... she wouldn't be. And nobody seemed to care. She couldn't help but think of all the wasted hours of trying to befriend them. Clearing the lump from her throat, she gave a small wave. "Bye, everyone!" she called, earning a few waves in return.

An odd mixture of relief and anxiety washed over Gretchen as the door shut behind her. She ran the back of her wrist over her eyes as she approached the car.

"What's wrong, dear?" Brontë's ears wiggled at her. In fact, all of the llamas leaned over the side of the trailer to nuzzle her as she passed.

Gretchen rubbed each llama's nose in turn. "Nothing's wrong. Everything is fine... besides the fact that we'll be fighting Eels in a few days. That's a bit stressful."

The others nodded.

"We've got a while before the arcade closes. Want to see my apartment?" she asked.

"Of course!" said Melville as the others murmured their agreement.

"Okay."

Gretchen returned to her car and slowly, carefully, inched from the parking spot, rattling the trailer. She happened to look up at the vet clinic right as her boss and her coworkers plastered themselves to the window with wide eyes. Faintly, in the reflection on the glass, Gretchen caught sight of the llamas staring back at them, tongues sticking out. She laughed and pulled back onto the street.

"All clear!" Gretchen called, beckoning the herd through her apartment door. They'd ditched the car and trailer on the street, and now, Neel's bucket in hand, she stealthily led the way through bushes, behind the dumpster, across the parking lot, and to her doorstep. The llamas weren't quite as stealthy as she was. They galloped after her, crashing through bushes and walking openly, unconcerned that any landlords might take issue with a herd of ungulates wandering the property. Melville hung back as the others filed through the door. He surveyed the area with unmistakable disdain curling his lips. "You live here?"

Gretchen tried to wave him through the door, but to her irritation, he ignored the gesture.

"It doesn't seem very safe."

"Melville, I swear. If someone sees us, it's not going to be fun." Neel's bucket felt heavier by the second.

"I can't believe you would pick *this* over staying with us," he huffed, finally moving across the threshold and stepping around the pile of shoes. Gretchen closed and locked the door.

"This place is a mess," Melville observed.

"I wasn't expecting company," she muttered, joining the herd in the common area. She set Neel's bucket by her feet and put her hands on her hips. Six llamas made the space extremely cramped, even without the little piles of junk littering the floor. She nudged a stack of board games against the wall with her foot, wishing she'd tidied up before leaving for the farm. "We should get rest before we head to the arcade," she said. "My bedroom is a lot smaller, so this might be the best place for you to sleep."

Neel gave her a pointed stare, but the llamas were too busy examining the room to answer. Austen, who stood beside the bookshelf, observed a shelf full of photographs. Her nose brushed against a framed picture of Gretchen and her college roommates. Austen squinted at the photo. "Are these your friends?"

"Yeah. I mean, they were. Everyone moved off in

different directions after we graduated, and it got hard to keep up with each other."

"Who are your friends now?"

Gretchen shrugged. "I'm starting to think adults don't have friends."

"Nonsense!" said Verne. "Everyone needs a herd."

Gretchen bit her lip. "I guess there's Harley, but I don't think he likes me very much."

"He's the one who's opening the training facility for us?" Austen asked.

"Yes."

"You should tell him how you feel."

She shook her head. "I'm going to scrounge up some pillows and blankets for you guys," she said, edging toward her bedroom. The door clicked as she shut it behind her and she let out a long breath. "Who knew llamas could be so judgmental," she muttered, moving to her closet to pull out some old blankets. The llamas probably didn't need them, but it was nice to be able to breathe for a moment without anyone telling her she was doing life wrong.

The plastic stars on her ceiling glowed faintly in the low light. Gradually, the stress from the trip ebbed, and she allowed the familiarity of her bedroom to comfort her. Clothes were strewn everywhere from her hasty packing job before she left for the farm. She began picking them up and folding them. The normalcy of the action felt strange after everything that had happened in the past week, and she could almost, *almost* pretend that no talking llamas stood outside her door. But memories of cutting into giant Space Eel guts made her nose wrinkle. There was no denying reality.

The thought of the coming invasion sent shivers down her spine. She hoped her hunch was right about the power source. If anything in the arcade had been made to power a shrink ray, it was that lava lamp. The thing always hummed and glowed, yet it had no power cord, and she'd never seen anyone change the batteries. It would make everything so much simpler if the Eels were all Neel's size.

Neel!

Horror gripped her as she realized that she'd left him alone with the herd. Dropping the blouse in her hand, she yanked the door open and stumbled into the living room. The herd lay in a cluster on the rug, chatting lightly with each other. She wandered over to the bucket by the door. Relief washed over her as Neel glared up at her with his usual silent demeanor.

"Gretchen! Want to come sit with us for a bit before we nap?" called Shelley.

She smiled. "Yeah."

They stayed up an hour more, talking and winding down. Gretchen's mind kept straying to thoughts of farm life. She imagined accepting Melville's offer. She also imagined refusing it. The imaginary scenario didn't go over very well. She had a feeling that the herd wouldn't let her go as easily as her coworkers had.

At last, Gretchen carried Neel back to her bedroom, set an alarm on her phone, and crawled under her covers.

16: S.A.L.T.

THE NEON SIGN of the Space Alien Laser Tag Arcade was dark when Gretchen and the herd arrived. Only one car sat in the lot, so Gretchen parked sideways across several spaces. Her heart beat fast as she climbed out of the car and locked Neel inside.

"Stay here. I need to warn Harley about you so he doesn't freak out," she said to the others. She threw several glances over her shoulder as she made her way into the building.

The comfortable sights and smells of the arcade greeted her when she stepped inside. The games were all quiet, as if sleeping, and the regular lights were on instead of the blacklights, but still, the place felt like home. Gretchen's eyes moved to the door of the laser tag room, and she found that the pedestal beside it was devoid of its usual lava lamp.

The creak of a door hinge swinging drew her

attention, and a familiar voice came from behind the refreshments counter. "I can't fathom why the hell you need to play laser tag at one o'clock in the morning."

A smile spread over Gretchen's face as she approached and propped her elbows on the counter's sticky surface. "I'm mad at you."

"Yeah? Is that why you're trying to get me fired?" Harley asked, returning the smile. "How's farm life treating you?"

"You'd know if you bothered to talk to me every once in a while." The words slipped out before she could stop them, and both of their smiles faded. For a moment, she considered laughing and throwing in a sarcastic joke to make him laugh too, but no. The conversation needed to happen, so she held her tongue.

"What do you mean?" Harley asked, though his tone made it obvious that he knew what she meant.

"Why don't you ever text me first?" Gretchen said past the lump, which had suddenly formed in her throat. "It really hurts, y'know, and it makes me feel like a desperate loser when I sit around, waiting for you to respond."

"I'm not making you sit around and wait," he countered.

"Harley," Gretchen hissed.

He cast his eyes to the sticky, starry floor and

shrugged. "I just figure that you don't need to be friends with me."

She arched an eyebrow. "That's a jerky thing to say."

"No," he said, waving his hand. "What I mean to say is... You have plans. You have goals. You're going to get into vet school and become a veterinarian. Look at me. I have half an astronomy degree that I walked away from, no intentions of going back, and I'm working at an arcade. I'm a bad example and I don't want to hold you back."

Gretchen crossed her arms. "You're really stupid," she said. "I'm not a puppet and you're not my all-knowing mentor."

"I know," said Harley, looking as if he wanted to melt through the floor.

"I don't want you to make decisions on our friend-ship without letting me have any input, because that sucks."

"Okay," he said.

"Okay," said Gretchen. She held out a hand, and Harley tentatively took it. She drew him into an awkward hug.

"Uh... You said you brought friends with you?"

A grin lit her face. "You should probably sit down for this... You're gonna flip when you meet them."

"You're really making it hard for me to let go of my escaped convict idea."

She shrugged as she backed out of the room. "Think more along the lines of alien llamas."

HARLEY'S JAW dropped when Gretchen, Neel's bucket clutched in one hand, led Melville and the others into the arcade.

"No!" he said. "Absolutely, not. Get them out!"

Melville walked up to him, wiggling his ears curiously, and spoke. "Harley, I presume?"

Harley leaned against the counter, as if about to pass out.

Gretchen hefted Neel onto its surface and moved to support her friend. "Harley, meet Melville."

"Melville talks," he said faintly.

Melville snorted. "He's not very bright, is he?"

"Hush," said Brontë. "You're being rude."

Harley wilted in Gretchen's arms. "Let's go get the laser tag gear," she said, pushing him back to his feet and steering him into the equipment room. She noted the empty pedestal as they passed it. Once the door swung shut behind them, Harley turned to face her with round eyes.

"They talk."

"I know," she said patiently. "It freaked me out, too. They told me they were abducted by aliens, but really, they got experimented on by scientists who wanted them to fight aliens and—"

"Please stop talking," he cut in. "I need to process one thing at a time."

"Fair."

A row of numbered vests and laser blasters lined two of the opposing walls in the room. Gretchen ran her finger along the numbers until she came to her preferred set, and pulled it off the rusted hook. "Where's the lava lamp?" she asked as she pulled the vest over her head.

Harley turned his back as she dressed herself and mumbled something under his breath. At first, it seemed like he wasn't going to answer her, so she repeated the question. He gave a small cough and scuffed the toe of his shoe against the tile. "About that... I hid it."

Gretchen blinked. "What?"

She moved to where she could see his face, and a blush stole over his cheeks.

"I got irritated about coming to work in the middle of the night for you, and..." He awkwardly rubbed the back of his head with one hand and waved the other. "You said you needed practice, anyway, so you shouldn't be mad! You should be thanking me."

Gretchen gaped and gave a laugh of disbelief. "That's so dumb! I told you I need it!" she protested, snapping the buckles into place.

Mischief lit his features. "Trust me. You already know where it is."

"You put it in the Eel's mouth, didn't you?"

"Did I?" he said, wiggling his eyebrows. "I'll have you know, it was quite the experience removing it from its pedestal. I can't believe everyone's assumed it's a lamp all these years."

Gretchen stuck her tongue out at him and picked out more equipment sets. She went for the larger sizes, hoping she could find a sensible way to attach them to the llamas without stretching them. The colorful vests definitely wouldn't fit around their torsos, but they could probably be fastened around their necks. The yellow and green striped blasters could then be tucked into the arm holes. They wouldn't be functional, but at least the llamas would be able to keep track of their health meters.

Once she'd looped the sixth vest over her arm, she took her burden back out to the main area. Harley followed.

"Do we have to wear those?" Shelley asked, ears slicked back against her head. She watched Gretchen slide the equipment off her arm and onto the bench by the cubbies.

"Yes. To know if the Eels kill you or not," Gretchen said, sending a nervous shudder through the herd. "Don't worry—the Eels in there are cardboard. But they'll shoot lasers at you with a stupid amount of accuracy."

Harley, overcoming his shock, gave a dry laugh as

he picked up a vest and approached Brontë. "It's only stupid accurate because you hesitate," he said.

"I do not," she huffed, equipping Shelley, then Austen. She was pleased at how snugly they fit.

"This reminds me too much of training days," muttered Verne, allowing her to wrap a vest around his neck.

Gretchen nodded and clicked the strap's buckles into place. "That's exactly what this is," she said. "We're practicing in a safe environment before we go out and fight Eels that could actually eat us." She slid the matching blaster into one of the arm holes and gave his neck a reassuring pat.

A commotion by the cubbies drew her attention. Harley tripped over a bench as he attempted to strap the last vest around Melville's neck, but the stubborn llama resisted, backing away and glaring. Gretchen watched with amusement until she realized that Melville looked prepared to spit. She stepped between them and took the vest from Harley's hands. "You want to fire up the game so we can get this show on the road?"

"Okay," he said, a note of relief in his voice. He walked backwards to the laser tag room without taking his eyes off Melville. "Don't let them destroy anything."

Gretchen gave Melville a warning scowl and clicked his vest into place. "Behave."

She led the herd into the darkened laser tag area. She could hear Harley starting up the systems.

"And it's a go," he said, pulling a lever.

The llamas watched in awe as the arcade flared to life. Bright, colorful lights swept over the room, revealing painted plywood cutouts of cows and barns. A model of a crashed UFO took up most of the center of the room. Their ears twitched as EDM pulsed through the air, its booming bass and fast tempo setting the herd on edge. Twain leapt a few inches off the floor as a clump of cardboard elvers rose from a hole in a foam meteorite, antennae flashing with colorful lights.

"How are we supposed to train with all this noise?" Melville yelled.

"You get used to it!" Gretchen yelled back. "We won't be fighting the real Eels in perfect silence anyway, so it will only make you better!"

"Really?" Austen also yelled.

Gretchen powered up her blaster. "I don't know, but it's more fun with the music!"

She beckoned the herd to huddle up. "There are twenty elvers in this room. I'm not telling you where they are, so you need to stay on your toes." She glanced at their artiodactylous feet, the corners of her lips twitching into a smile as she said this.

Melville frowned, clearly unamused, but didn't say anything. Gretchen pointed to the elvers. "Whenever you see one, bop it with your nose, but no spitting! We don't want to get Harley in trouble."

"What do we do once we've tagged them all?" Brontë asked.

Gretchen's expression became serious. "When we actually face the Eels, it's important we stick together, so wait at the door until we are all accounted for. After that, we move to the next room."

"What's in there?" asked Shelley.

But Gretchen shook her head. "We take it one room at a time. Also, we need to look for the power source. It's in one of the rooms."

"Where?" asked Melville.

"I don't know."

His expression became grumpier. "What's it look like?"

"A lava lamp."

His ears swiveled until they lay almost flat against his head. "There's no way we're going to find it *and* beat the Eels if we stay clumped together. It would be more prudent to—"

"No!" Gretchen cut him off. Fear flashed in the whites of the others' eyes. She waved to focus their attention back on her before they could overthink things. "We don't leave anyone behind."

"Are you guys ready yet?" Harley called from the console. "I don't want to send the rest until you're done talking."

"One minute!" she said, then addressed the herd again, making sure to meet each set of bulbous, heavily-lashed, glowing green eyes. "Twenty Eels. No spit. Stay together."

She waved at Harley, who gave her a thumbs up. He pressed a few buttons on the console and a wave of elvers swooped past the herd.

Cries of terror went up and the llamas bolted behind a large foam rock.

"Hey!" Gretchen ran after them in confusion. "What's this all about? We haven't even started!"

"YOU DIDN'T SAY WE WERE FIGHTING *THESE* EELS," Melville snarled.

"*What?!*" Gretchen cried. "They're not real!"

The other llamas trembled fearfully and flinched as the elvers passed again. "We used to fight these when the aliens were training us," said Twain.

"They're awful," said Shelley.

Gretchen hid her shock. She'd have to look into the origins of the arcade later. "They're cardboard," she said, reaching out and tapping on one. It wobbled flimsily. "They can't hurt you. And look—" She raised her blaster and shot the target on Twain's vest.

"Hey!" he cried as his health meter lost a bar.

"Did that hurt?" she asked.

"No," he grumbled.

"They won't hurt you either. They just look scary," she said, pointing after the elvers. She pointed to the room. "This is where you're allowed to make mistakes. If you run out of bars, you don't even have to leave the room. It's practice."

The llamas peered anxiously through the door, but didn't protest.

"You're my friends. You trust me, right?" Gretchen asked.

They nodded.

"Okay. Let's do this."

At her signal, they turned back and charged through the door.

17: Telekinetic

Einstein was having a bad night. After Gretchen and the others left, he returned to the dining room and took a closer look at the documents from his file. Tears welled in his big brown eyes as he read:

> Cria 002 has taken to the prototype helmet. He is now moving objects half his size using only the telekinetic energy generated by the device.

He pulled away, trembling. "No. It must be referencing a different llama," he said. But his words felt flat, even to his own ears.

"How dare she dredge all this up. Elsie never asked us to remember."

Elsie had told them they didn't have to remember.

That there was a different plan and that they no longer had to fight. But that was before she'd died, and before Melville had seen the eggs in the ditch. The herd had done their best to destroy them, but they'd known the others were coming. The others were coming, and Elsie had not imparted knowledge of her backup plan on any of them. The boxes of shrink ray parts taunted him from where they sat on the table. Einstein drew in a deep breath and pictured the large gear sticking out of one rising into the air. As hard as he concentrated, all he managed to do was strain a muscle in his neck.

"Telekinesis, yeah right..." he huffed, skulking from the room. "Gretchen is wrong about the aliens. *Scientists*," he corrected himself. "They don't want to protect us. They probably want us to get eaten. Satiate the monsters so they, themselves, can be spared." He slipped Melville's door hook over his neck before he exited the house. "I need to take a walk."

Only a sliver of the moon shone between the clouds, watching through its heavily-lidded eye as Einstein made his way down the road. Wind whispered through trees and grasses, setting him on edge. He wished Gretchen had never opened that folder. Knowing the aliens had been Earth scientists all along almost made things worse.

The silhouette of the laboratory brought him an inkling of relief. The past few weeks, Melville had said over and over that there was no better way to fight off dread of the Eel attack than to keep an eye on their approaching enemies. He strode across the empty parking lot and let himself into the building.

The hollow sound of his hoofsteps against tile echoed in the hallway as he came to the control room door. Metal scraped against metal, causing his teeth to grate as he hooked the door to the control room open. The comfortable *whirs* and *hums* of machinery surrounded him, and he hummed back as he approached the console and scanned the screen. Only clouds. He shivered as the tension left his muscles.

"I should get home," he said once he'd regained his composure.

Einstein closed the door behind him and cast a glance down the hallway. To his surprise, the door at its end sat slightly ajar. That door had always been locked before. A thousand questions swirled through his mind. Placing one hesitant hoof in front of the other, he approached the room, stuck his nose through the crack, and pulled it open.

Lights snapped on.

Einstein found himself in a space twice the size of the control room, lined with shelves, tables, and pedestals. It reminded him of a library, not that he'd ever been in a library. He stepped inside, casting a cautious glance over the area, but he was alone.

To his right sat a wooden desk with a book lying open on top. A list of names and reference numbers were written in two columns, and he wondered if it might be some sort of card catalog system. He'd read about that in a book Elsie had brought him once. As he scanned the columns, his neck pressed into the back of a chair pushed neatly beneath the desk. None of the names rang a bell, and with an impatient snort, he moved on.

A row of pedestals took up the adjacent wall. Strange, but interesting objects were arranged on each, and Einstein cursed the lack of labels or signs. He peered into the silver sphere on top of the first, but couldn't determine its purpose aside from causing the hair on his snout to prickle. The next pedestal held a helmet of sorts, made of wide bands of metal. A couple of antennae stuck out from the top. With some difficulty, Einstein maneuvered it to the edge of the platform.

With a sinuous motion of his neck, he slipped the helmet on.

Clarity washed over his mind in an instant, and with it, came a tidal wave of memories.

HE STOOD, *shivering, surrounded by the glass walls of his classroom as a cyclops dressed in white adjusted the helmet to fit his head.*

"Please don't throw me to the monsters," he pleaded again.

The cyclops said nothing.

"I don't want to fight them. They're scary."

Another cyclops who was arranging objects on a table let out a sigh. "You're not participating in battle training today, 002. You're helping us test a new piece of equipment."

Einstein felt himself relax. He was led toward the table, where six cubes sat in a perfectly straight line.

"Alright, 002. I want you to clear your mind and concentrate on moving these cubes."

EINSTEIN BLINKED as the memory faded and the room came back into view. The table with the cubes was nowhere to be seen, but his eye caught on a set of keys, hanging from a hook on the wall. He drew in a deep breath, and concentrated.

The keys twitched.

THE FIRST CUBE clattered to the floor as Einstein leapt back, startled. "It moved! I moved it!" he exclaimed.

One cyclops chuckled. "Well done. Let's try again, but this time, try to hold it in the air for a longer time. Think you can handle a full minute?"

Einstein eagerly nodded.

. . .

Very gently, he lifted the keys from the hook, and set them into orbit around the room.

"Amazing," he whispered, following them with his eyes. As they flew past the row of pedestals, he picked the silver sphere up, too. Then the chair behind the desk. He guided them with relative ease, though he didn't think adding a fourth object would go overly well. He'd never mastered picking up all six cubes.

Memories of the hours upon hours he'd practiced this with the cyclopes continued flooding back as if he had never forgotten. He would've said it was like riding a bicycle, except for the fact that he didn't know how to ride a bicycle. "Scientists," he corrected himself once more, sending the sphere in circles around the chair. "Gretchen said they were scientists."

As gently as he'd lifted the objects, he set them back in their proper places. The euphoria wore off, and a worried thought crept into his head. "How could I have forgotten all that?" Einstein shook his tail and began to explore the room, this time more animatedly, telekinetically opening cabinets and drawers as he passed. The helmet wobbled atop his head, slipping over his eyes every time he went to peer into a drawer. "I'll get Gretchen to tighten it when she returns," he decided.

In one of the display cases along the back wall, he found a box full of what looked to be miniature, hand-held shrink rays, exactly like the one in the blueprints, though, a lot more colorful. The lime green stripes decorating their bright, yellow barrels were a nice touch. He mentally reached out to open the case and picked up the entire box.

"Gretchen will be pleased to have these!"

He came to a display case with a cloth draped over it. With a deft motion, Einstein focused on a fold and swept the material off the glass. It billowed, then crumpled into a pile on the floor, leaving the llama to stare in horror at what lay beneath the glass. The skull of a monster smiled back at him. Its pointed teeth protruded from its jaws in neat rows. A distressed hum rattled his throat as he instinctively took a few steps back from the hideous thing. Memories he had been fighting back for years now surfaced.

"PLEASE, I don't want to go in there!" Einstein cried. His legs felt like jelly, and he struggled to draw in air.

"You'll be fine," the cyclops reassured. It was the one with the higher voice. "We won't let them hurt you."

"They're so fast, and they have so many teeth!"

He squealed as he was given a gentle push toward the shadowy doorway.

"You're fast, too. And you can spit."

He gasped as he was pushed through the door and the curtain of rubbery strips parted around him to reveal the darkness of the adjacent room. Slowly, Einstein's eyes adjusted, and his night vision kicked in. A pulse of light from overhead all but blinded him, and he raised his head to stare into the giant, toothy maw of a monster. The jaw snapped shut with a mechanical squeal and steadily opened again. A deafening shriek shook the walls of the room, drowning out Einstein's own screams.

THE DROP CLOTH flew through the air and wrapped itself over the display case once again. Einstein bolted from the room without a backward glance. The box of mini shrink rays floated behind him, trailing as if attached to a string.

18: Tag

"It's gotta be in the Eel," Gretchen muttered. "Harley sucks at hiding things. I *know* he hid it in the big one." All the same, she peered into the crevice of a foam asteroid, and leapt back as a couple of cardboard elvers popped out.

Pew! Pew!

Their lights faded as they were hit, and they lowered again. She smiled smugly and added another mental tick mark to her tally. Ten. Her smile widened when she glanced at the timer overhead and realized she'd reached a new personal record.

The herd was faring pretty well, too. Once they'd concluded that the goofy cutouts couldn't hurt them, they'd loosened up and eagerly sought out their targets. Harley, watching from the surveillance screen in the control booth, had been toggling off the elver mechanisms as the llamas bopped them with their noses.

"Find anything?" Shelley called over the music as she turned and galloped toward Gretchen.

Gretchen shook her head. "How's your health meter looking?"

Shelley craned her neck to peer at the top of her blaster. "I only lost one bar so far!"

"I think we've cleared the room of elvers. I can't find any more," called Verne from somewhere up ahead.

"Has anyone found the power source?" came Brontë's voice from around a plywood cow.

"Gather up!" Gretchen said, waving her arm. "Nice job with the Eels. I'm loving the teamwork, everyone. I think it's time to move to the next room."

Palpable apprehension settled over the group.

"We're not ready," Melville said, stepping forward.

"Yes, you are. Look at what we just did."

"I feel ready," said Austen. "This is much less scary than when we were younger."

"I'm ready, too," said Twain. "This was a piece of cake."

"Let's cut through here," Gretchen said, beckoning them toward a curtain that hung over the entrance to the next room. She slipped through the heavy, black velvet and was gripped by the sensation of falling as a starry void engulfed her.

The illusion never failed to take her breath away. Judging by the gasps and hums behind her, she wasn't alone in her discombobulation. Regaining balance, she stepped out into the star-speckled simulation of outer space. Mirrors lined the walls, ceiling, and floor, reflecting the strings of fairy lights which hung all around in endless repetition.

Gretchen shook off her amazement and waded through the sea of stars to the center of the room. The muted EDM pulsed faintly, and she could clearly hear the hoofsteps of the llamas echoing against the glass. At the end of the tunnel, Gretchen pushed through another velvety black curtain and came to the room on the other end.

The second room was a hellscape compared to the last one. Craggy rocks and ruins littered the floor, and everything was bathed in red light. The music became more ominous. The lights dimmed as a screech split the air. Someone bumped into Gretchen from behind and she stumbled forward a few steps. *ZAP!* She leapt back as a laser beam hit the ground at her feet. Over-head, an adult Eel retracted into a crevice in the wall, its red eyes flaring.

"You didn't say they would fight back," hissed Melville.

"We have to be prepared for anything," she said, urging the herd out of range as the Eel extended again. The laser flickered on the floor. The herd's attention was so focused on the bright dot that none of them noticed a tile on the floor sliding away. *POP!* Another Eel sprung from below, shooting Brontë with its laser. She shrieked, and Gretchen caught her before she could bolt.

"I take it back. I don't think I can do this," said Twain, voice wavering. "I want to go home."

"I want to go home too," said Austen.

"Agreed," said Verne.

More frightened murmurs rose from among the herd.

"Hey, hey!" Gretchen called, waving an arm and cutting them off. She took in their trembling forms, taking note of the way the whites of their eyes shone beneath the blacklights. Brontë trembled violently at her side. "We can't stop now. Look, I get it—when I first started playing, I was scared of everything, too. The lights, the music, the jump-scares... It's all over-whelming. But these Eels are fake, remember? What are you going to do when this is real? When the Eels attack Hildegard Farm, there will be no option to leave and go home. We will have to stand our ground and fight."

"But it's scary," said Shelley.

Gretchen's face softened. "I know it is. But we don't have a choice. Also, that thing's on a timer, so we should probably get a move on," she said, tilting her head at the loose tile and drawing a few anxious stares. "Let's find that lava lamp and get out of here," she said.

They moved forward with caution, dodging toothy Eels and startling whenever a laser lit up at their hooves. Occasionally, a laser would hit one of their vests, and the life meter would drop lower. Gretchen's heart beat faster. They were coming upon the part of the game that she always screwed up. She glanced at the timer and was relieved to see they still had a solid ten minutes left.

Austen shrieked as an Eel sprung from the ceiling and took another bar off her health meter. Up ahead, the terrain became rockier, and a glowing red chasm opened in the floor. Gretchen fell into a crouch and counted the seconds under her breath. Right on time, the whir of some large mechanism came from overhead, and down came the largest Eel in the entire game. It was easily triple the length of the others in the room, and it had fancier head ornamentation. With a metallic squeal, the jaws parted and a loud screech played over the speakers.

A swarm of elvers flew across the room, cellophane tails glittering as they spit lasers. Several hit Gretchen, and she watched in dismay as her health meter dropped a few bars. She could tell by her friends' cries that they'd been hit as well. They needed to find shelter. She could see a pile of asteroids up ahead, but they'd never make it before the elvers returned.

"Circle up!" she shouted, and the herd gathered with their backs to each other as the elvers swooped around for another attack.

Pew! Pew! Pew! Pew!

Lasers shot wildly through the room. Gretchen couldn't tell how many targets she'd hit, but she lost another bar on her meter. The llamas bopped as many as they could, and Gretchen trusted that Harley was watching close enough to toggle them off as they were hit.

"I'm down!" called Twain.

Several frightened bleats went up at his words, and the llamas pressed closer together to hide their own targets.

Gretchen eyed the elvers, and when they began moving away, she called out, "Run for the asteroids!"

The herd took off—Twain, more slowly, unsure if he should stay in the game or not. Before they reached safety, another screech shook the room and larger Eels rose from holes in the floor. Gretchen pushed herself to run faster. More yells and groans came from the herd as they were hit and their health meters dropped to zero.

Melville kept pace with Gretchen, and together, they slid behind the first asteroid they came to. They panted and leaned against the grimy foam.

"How many of us are left?" Melville gasped.

Gretchen looked over her shoulder. The other

llamas had settled in the middle of the floor, paying no attention to the prop monsters as they caught their breath.

"Looks like it's just you and me," she said.

The enormous Eel let out a threatening hiss. Gretchen poked her head above the asteroid and glared at it. She'd fought this Eel so many times before, but this time she knew it for what it was. *The Queen.* The lights flickered, bathing the entire room in an eerie red. The lights along the Queen's body blinked on and off in rapid succession. It was all so overwhelming that she nearly missed it. A soft green glow emanated from behind the Eel's teeth.

"I've never noticed that before," she muttered to herself before it clicked. *The lava lamp.* Gretchen silently cursed Harley. How the hell was she supposed to get it out of there? She tapped Melville's neck and pointed.

"What do we do?" he hissed.

Gretchen shrugged, feeling sweat trickling down her neck. Her eyes followed the length of the mechanical creature, searching for any weak point, but the thing seemed impenetrable.

"Could you at least try to shoot the light out?" Melville said, squinting against the brightness. "It's making it hard to think."

Gretchen peeked over the foam rock again, narrowing her eyes. "Ugh, this is horrible," she said.

She took a breath and, instead of aiming for the heart, she aimed for the flashing lure.

The lights in the room dimmed.

With a creaking groan, some mechanism in the ceiling lowered the Eel to the floor as the neon sign overhead flashed the green word: WINNER. Gretchen's heart raced as she hopped over the foam rock and ran to the defeated mechanical creature.

Her hands shook as she reached into its mouth and withdrew the lime green cylinder. It was odd. She'd seen it a thousand times before but had never paid it much attention. It hummed against her palms, radiating enough heat to make it a little uncomfortable to hold. Particles drifted through the gloopy medium inside, occasionally sparkling.

"I was right. This can't be anything other than the power source," she called toward the control room. "That was too easy. Did you put it in beginner mode?"

"No, you've just racked up loads of experience from wasting all your time and money on this dump," Harley's voice drawled over the loudspeaker.

Gretchen turned to find Melville and the others gathered behind her, tails wagging.

"It's not going to be that easy, is it?" said Twain.

"I'm afraid not," she said, tucking the cylinder under her arm and helping him pull the vest off his neck.

A disgruntled expression settled over Melville's

face as she did this. "Don't you think we should keep practicing?"

She shook her head. "That's enough for one night. We all need to rest."

Gretchen collected the vests and then led the llamas through the exit doors. Harley met them by the concessions stand. "That was the coolest thing I've seen... probably ever," he said. "What's all this for anyway?"

The truth burned on the end of her tongue, but she held back. Harley didn't need to get dragged into this. "Wouldn't you like to know?"

"Gretchen..."

"I want to tell you, but I can't. Not yet."

She retrieved Neel's bucket.

"What's in there?" Harley asked, looking in before Gretchen could stop him. He froze as he stared at Neel and Neel stared back at him. "That's an Eel. Gretchen... that's an *Eel*."

"His name is Neel, and I need to get going."

"Gretchen, wait, I need answers."

"Promise me if I... If I don't come back, you'll remember me fondly," she said.

"Gretchen, what's going on?" he said, laying a hand on her arm. "You're scaring me."

She cackled and pulled away. "I'll see you later, Harley."

19: RADAR

EINSTEIN LAY SPRAWLED in the dust outside the weather observation center where he'd tripped and collapsed after his mad dash from the library. His breath came in short gasps and his heart hammered painfully in his thoracic cavity until he felt like it would burst.

"Just a skull!" he gasped. "It was just a skull and it can't hurt me!"

Gradually, his breathing evened. Small clumps of grass tickled his legs, and above, the stars glinted ominously. Einstein pulled himself from his stupor and glanced back at the open door. His muscles shook and panic made his brain feel foggy, but he knew that running wouldn't solve anything. Fresh resolve burned in his veins as he forced himself to his hooves and walked back into the building, all the way to the end of the hall. The library door swung shut with a *click.*

A sudden ringing caused Einstein to jump. A telephone. The noise came from the direction of the front office. He carefully crept toward the door and pushed through it with ease. A large desk, strewn with papers, took up most of the space in the room. The telephone sat on its receiver beside a sleek computer monitor.

Ring ring.

Ring ring.

Einstein wasn't quite sure what made him do it—he supposed a part of him wished that Gretchen would be on the other end of the line to comfort him—but he knocked the phone from its dock and lowered his head to the receiver.

"Hello?"

"Hey, Joshua, it's Edgar," came a man's voice. "I was calling to see if you were in tonight. I know you've been sick, but I couldn't remember if you'd taken off again or not."

Einstein blinked. "I'm here."

"That's a relief, man. I want to come in, but Penelope and I are still tied up with Elsie's estate. The recipient wants to sell it, and of course everyone is harassing us about what will be done with it. We haven't caught a break all week."

Einstein couldn't think of what to say to that, so he responded with a simple, "Of course."

"And on top of that, her llamas have been acting

out. Did I tell you about how they broke into our building earlier this week?"

"No."

"Well, watch out for them tonight. We'll catch up soon. How's the weather looking? Anything out of the ordinary?"

Something about Edgar's tone caught Einstein off guard. It was almost like... *he knew.* A hum of surprise escaped the llama's throat.

"You okay, man? You still sound pretty sick."

Einstein pulled himself together and bent over the phone. "I'm fine. Everything looks fine," he said.

"Great. I need to get back to work, but call me if you need anything."

"I will."

Click. A monotonous tone droned after Edgar hung up.

Einstein reeled. Edgar knew. He knew about the invasion and he had never once said a word to Melville! All that man had told them at the funeral was to get lost. Had he known that Elsie knew? Had she been the one to tell him about the Eels? With wildly racing thoughts, Einstein turned and examined the papers on the desk. Most contained lists of coordinates, but a few grainy photographs were scattered throughout the pile. He squinted at them, but couldn't make out any recognizable form.

Finally, he returned to the control room. As his

thoughts settled, he felt calmer knowing that it wasn't only Gretchen and his herd who knew about the invasion. Pale light from the computer monitor bathed his wool as he stepped back through the door and approached the screen. The forecast showed clear skies. He picked out the little clump of red pixels representing Hildegard Farm and gave a contented hum.

The screen refreshed.

To Einstein's horror, a clump of cyan dots appeared on the far right side of the main screen. He touched his nose to the dots, and a little box popped up beside them.

ALTITUDE: 52,000 ft

The screen refreshed again.
The dots moved left.
The box updated.

ALTITUDE: 51,900 ft

Ice ran through his veins.

"They're here."

Einstein paced in front of the screen. The dots moved closer and closer to Hildegard Farm, and the altitude decreased at an alarming rate every time the map refreshed. He checked the wind direction and speed, did a few mental calculations, and determined they could arrive within the next twenty-four hours.

"Oh no," Einstein said, eyes rolling back in his head. "Oh no, oh no, oh no. I have to tell Gretchen."

He managed to remember the box of mini shrink rays before he galloped out of the building and down the street. It floated along beside him all the way back to the property and all the way into the house. When he finally set it down, exhaustion settled in his muscles, though he wasn't sure if it was from the mad sprint to the house or the telekinesis.

"The phone, the phone," he muttered frantically and headed toward the kitchen.

It hung on the wall, where Gretchen had shown him. At first, he tried dialing the number with his mind, but quickly found it to be tedious, ineffective, and requiring a far more delicate touch than he possessed at the moment. In the end, he knocked the phone from the dock with his nose, then clamped a pencil between his teeth and used the eraser to punch in the number.

"Hello?" he called into the phone as it swung on its cord.

Only the dial tone sounded back. Einstein drew in a deep breath and waited. After a moment, he heard a click.

"Hello?" The voice was garbled.

"Gretchen?" Einstein said into the phone, desperately hoping that the device was picking up his words.

"Hey!" He relaxed when he heard Gretchen's voice. It could've been wishful thinking, but she sounded a little bit like Elsie. "How's it going with the shrink ray?"

"Poorly. You need to come back now. Our projections were wrong. They're coming tomorrow."

The line went quiet.

"Are you still there?" he asked.

"Stay calm. We'll be back in the morning," Gretchen said.

"Hurry," he urged.

After she hung up, he left the phone dangling on its cord and walked nervous loops around the living room until he collided with the box of mini shrink rays. He must've dropped it when he came through the door.

"I should finish the big one before they get home," he said. "It will make Gretchen happy."

Einstein decided to move all the pieces of the giant laser to the barn, where he'd have more room to work. They floated weirdly behind him, then drifted to the floor. He lined them up against the wall and telekinetically pulled the pieces out, one by one.

By the time they were empty and the pieces of the laser lay strewn over every inch of the barn floor, Einstein's head throbbed painfully from the immense psychic effort. He sank to his knees and pored over the blueprints, willing the headache to go away. But as he tried to read, his eyelids drooped and his neck bent until the helmet slipped and fell crooked across his ears. Despite his struggles to stay awake, exhaustion won out and unconsciousness claimed him.

20: Roadside

"I TOLD YOU THIS WOULD HAPPEN," Melville said, sticking his nose in the air. His wool ruffled as cars sped past on the highway. The group had set out while the world was still cloaked in darkness. They'd been driving for an hour, and still, the sun had not risen. Turning to the rest of the herd, he said, "Didn't I tell her we needed to pull over two miles ago?"

The others kept quiet, shifting nervously and watching the road.

"Shut up, Melville, I need to think," said Gretchen, massaging her temples. The incessant clicking of the hazard lights wore on her nerves. She'd pulled onto the shoulder of the road as soon as her car's front tire had blown, and now paced, considering her options. She could take it to a shop and get told off for being stupid, or call a roadside service and be told off for being stupid. Either way, she'd have to have an excuse ready for why she was hauling a herd of llamas with her beat-up car. "I think we can make it to an auto shop on the spare," she finally said.

"Do you know how to put it on?" Melville said, leaning over her shoulder.

"I don't need your attitude," she said, pushing past him to open the trunk. She found the spare beneath an old ratty blanket and pulled it out. It took a few moments of rummaging to find the jack and the wrench. She'd never changed a tire before but was sure she could figure it out.

She knelt, wrench in hand, and began loosening the lug nuts. The llamas kept watch as she worked, and soon, she had the car lifted, and on went the spare. As she lowered the car, a jeep pulled onto the shoulder and parked behind the trailer, its own hazards blinking. A short, dark-haired woman with a sharp nose stepped out of the vehicle and approached the scene. She looked as if she had dressed to hike, with sturdy boots, a weathered brown jacket, and a scarf around her neck. If the llamas surprised her, she didn't show it.

"Need a hand?"

Gretchen opened her mouth to decline, but a glint caught her eye. A small compass glittered from where it adorned the woman's jacket.

Gretchen met her eyes. "Yes."

The woman smiled. "I've done this many times—

once during a monsoon in Africa, even—but never did I have a trailer full of llamas with me." She reached to stroke Shelley's neck, then joined Gretchen by the car. "Oh! Looks like you don't need me. You got it."

"I did," Gretchen shrugged. "But it's not going to get me back to my farm, and I don't know how to explain the reckless trailering to a mechanic."

"I see." She looked thoughtful. "How about I go get you a tire and help you put it on so that we don't have to deal with any pesky, prying questions."

Gretchen blinked. "That's really nice of you. You don't even know me."

"We explorers have to stick together. So you'll accept my help?"

Gretchen hesitated, but then nodded. "I normally wouldn't ask a stranger to go so far out of their way for me, but yes. It's important for me to get back as soon as possible. It's an emergency."

She winked. "Understood."

The woman returned to her jeep. "It will probably take an hour for me to get back. Hang tight until then!"

Gretchen waved awkwardly and turned to pull open her car door. She grabbed her sketchbook from her messenger bag and opened it to a blank page. If she had to be stuck here for another hour, she might as well make a list. "Gather up, everyone!" she called, motioning for the herd to join her.

"Who was that?" Austen asked.

"No clue," she said. "But we need to make a game plan. The Eels could arrive at any time in the next twelve hours." She made a few notes in her book. "I was thinking we should lure them to one spot, trap them, and attack."

"How?" Twain asked.

"For one, we need to pick an accessible spot away from the house. That shouldn't be hard to find." She wrote out the task and drew a box beside it. "Two, we need a good way to attract them." Her tongue poked between her teeth as she wrote. "Any ideas?"

"Meat," said Shelley at the same time that Verne said, "lights."

"Exactly what I was thinking," Gretchen agreed, writing both down.

"Three. Attack with the shrink ray."

"We should really just kill them," said Melville.

"Shut up. And four. Gather them. We can keep them in a jar or something and then donate them to a zoo." She drew in a deep breath. "Four steps. We've got this."

"I don't feel like we've got this," said Twain.

Gretchen set her sketchbook aside and took his face in her hands. She looked into his dark eyes. "You do. There's something else I need to tell you."

The llamas waited with pricked ears and bated breath. Even Melville's attention was riveted on her.

"As you know, I read through your files that I got from the lab. Those scientists worked hard to give you a fighting chance against the Eels. Einstein was the only one they trained in telekinesis, but you have several mutations, like a high degree of intelligence, enhanced agility, night vision, and..." she paused for dramatic effect, "your spit is corrosive." Her words hung in the air, and when the llamas didn't react, she continued on. "It's produced in a special gland in the roof of your mouth. The file didn't say anything about how to get it to release the acid, but I'm sure if you experiment—"

"We know," Brontë interrupted in an amused tone.

"What?" said Gretchen.

"It's pretty nasty stuff. It can eat away at metal."

Gretchen turned to Melville with disbelief. Her voice pitched. "You knew that, and you *spit at me?*"

Melville huffed, but wouldn't meet her eyes. "I didn't use the acid spit, just the regular kind," he mumbled.

She waved away her irritation. "I'm hoping Einstein will have the shrink ray up and running by the time we get back. If not, we'll reevaluate. But for now, let's get that spare removed."

AN HOUR LATER, the stranger's jeep returned to its place behind the trailer. The woman hopped out of the driver's side and retrieved a tire from the trunk. Gretchen stood from where she sat in the grass and awkwardly watched her roll the tire toward her car.

"Thank you so, so much. I don't have any cash on me, but—"

The woman cut her off. "Don't worry about it. The guy at the shop owed me a big favor."

"Oh."

"Here, help me get this on," she said.

The llamas crowded around to watch as Gretchen stooped and helped tighten the lug nuts. She stole occasional glances at the woman, trying to remember if she'd seen her at the funeral, but nothing about her rang any bells. After the tire was secured, they removed the jack and got to their feet.

"Seriously, *thank you,*" said Gretchen. "I want to repay you somehow."

A smile spread over the woman's face. She stroked a few of the llamas' necks before starting toward her jeep. Gretchen and the herd followed.

"You can repay me by getting back to your farm and helping the next explorer who comes along," the woman said.

Gretchen watched her climb into the driver's seat. "Did you know Elsie?" she finally worked up the courage to ask.

Her smile got bigger. "Not personally, but I met her briefly at a few meetings. You've got her spunk."

"Meetings? For work?"

But the woman only laughed and started her jeep. "Good luck with whatever adventure you're on. Perhaps I'll see you at a meeting someday." She pulled away before Gretchen could ask any more questions.

"That was wild," said Melville.

"Almost as wild as talking llamas," Gretchen agreed. "C'mon. We have an invasion to stop."

21: Close Encounter

WHEN EINSTEIN CAME TO, the world had already begun to stir. "Oh no," he said, pushing himself to his hooves. "I wasn't supposed to fall asleep." He dashed out of the barn, hoping to be met with the sight of Gretchen's car, but the driveway remained as empty as it had been during the night. His head tilted upward, but the graying sky appeared empty as well. A few birds called from the woods and the chirping of crickets swelled from the fields, but this did little to reassure him. The whole farm felt too open, too exposed, and he, too unprepared.

"Where is everyone?" he murmured.

He galloped to the house, feeling like monsters could descend from the sky at any moment and shatter the stillness.

Inside, the house was just as he had left it the night before, except he couldn't find the pencil he'd used to dial the phone. He searched the floor and the kitchen countertop, but saw no sign of it. Finally, he gave up and went to Elsie's room, where Gretchen had been studying. "Aha!" he said, as he spotted a few pencils and highlighters in a pile along with various papers and scraps.

As he bent to pick one up, he caught sight of a crumpled napkin with the words *Billy, your neighbor,* along with a phone number scrawled across it. He nosed it aside, chose his writing utensil, and returned to the kitchen.

Grasping the pencil in his teeth, he dialed Gretchen's number. The tone sounded, but she didn't pick up. Einstein huffed in frustration. Outside, the sky continued to grow lighter and the fact that he hadn't finished building the shrink ray weighed heavier and heavier on his mind.

"I haven't even started," he said, pacing across the living room. "I have to start."

He tried to bolt from the house, but collided with none other than Priscilla.

Einstein shrieked.

So did Priscilla.

"Whoah, whoah!" she cried, holding her hands out as if to calm him. "What the hell?! Where's Gretchen?"

Einstein let the first syllable slip before he caught himself and ended up awkwardly humming. Priscilla pulled the helmet from his head. She turned it over in her hands, taking in the wires and sensors. "What has she been doing to you?"

The woman stroked his neck comfortingly. "Don't worry. She'll be gone soon and *I'll* take care of you."

She put a hand on his back and led him in the direction of the paddock and the barn. "I'm so glad I stopped by to check in on things. This is no way to run a farm."

The closer they got, the more Einstein panicked. He couldn't allow Priscilla to see the inside of the barn. Thoughts of making a run for it crossed his mind, but she had his helmet, and without it, he wouldn't be able to finish the shrink ray. His steps slowed, but she pushed him along. Once inside the paddock, he dug his hooves into the ground and refused to move. Priscilla offered him a sweet smile. "You must be so tired and confused."

Einstein was both tired and confused, but not for the reasons she thought. He eyed the helmet in her hands.

"I can't believe Gretchen is using this place for a science experiment." She examined the helmet again, eyebrows knitting together as she ran her thumbs along the sensors. "This is animal abuse! Well, it stops here. Let me feed you and then I'll go track down my no-good cousin and give her a piece of my mind."

She tucked the helmet under her arm and started toward the barn.

"Uhhhhhhh..." Einstein said, following her.

"Of course she left the barn doors hanging open, too. This disgusts me. The sooner she's gone, the better. I knew—" Priscilla fell quiet as she took in the odd instruments littering the floor. She bent and picked up the blueprints. "What the—"

The helmet and blueprints went flying as Einstein headbutted her. "HEY!" she cried, stumbling backward.

Einstein continued to advance and lash out, causing the woman to back out of the barn, repeatedly yelling, "What's gotten into you?" Her cry morphed into, "What has Gretchen done to you?"

Once she was completely clear of the barn, she turned and fled the paddock. The gate rattled as she slammed it shut and locked it. "I'm telling Penelope! I'm going to save you! The madness stops here!"

Einstein panted as he watched her retreat to her car and drive away. "This isn't good."

He would have to work fast if he wanted to beat the Eels *and* Priscilla. He made his way back to the barn and nudged the blueprints with a hoof. The complexity of it made his head spin. "I wish Verne were here to help."

Verne wasn't here. But as the name and number on the napkin crossed Einstein's mind, an idea began to form. Perhaps he did need a helper. A helper with thumbs. He slipped the helmet back on his head and galloped back to the house. After checking the number on the napkin again, he dialed it into the phone. It took a few rings before the recipient answered.

"This is Billy," came the familiar gruff voice.

Einstein cleared his throat, but his mind went blank. What was he supposed to say?

"Hello?"

"Hi! Hello!" Einstein mentally kicked himself. He strained his voice until it scratched and creaked. He knew he didn't necessarily need to disguise his voice, but he wanted to sell the part. "This is Gretchen's grandfather."

"Well, howdy! I didn't know you were in the area, or else I would've offered to invite you for a beer. Everything alright?"

"Everything is fine. I'm actually working on a project and could use an extra set of hands. Would you like to come over and take a look?"

"Sure! I'll be right over!"

As soon as they hung up, Einstein retrieved a cloak and a walker from the garage and moved to the front of the house. He decided not to open the door quite yet, in case his appearance would be a deterrent. A few minutes later, the roar of an engine sounded, and Billy's truck came into view through the window as it pulled up the driveway.

Billy hopped out of the driver's side, clutching a large toolbox in one hand and a case of beer in the other. As he approached, Einstein could see his faded black t-shirt with a green Martian printed on the front, and the red flannel over it. He also noted that his toolbox was plastered with stickers depicting Bigfoot, the Loch Ness Monster, and Mothman. This would be too easy. He telekinetically opened the door as Billy stepped onto the porch.

Billy's face blanched. "Are you the Grim Reaper?" His wide eyes filled with fear as they took in Einstein's looming form. "I'm not ready to go. I... I won't go." His knees bent as if he were preparing to run.

Einstein's own knees wobbled under the weight of the cloak as he leaned against the walker. He hated the disguise that Verne had engineered for the herd, but, he admitted, it was effective.

"I am not the Grim Reaper. I am Gretchen's grand-father," the llama said.

Billy somewhat relaxed, but looked him up and down skeptically. "Give an old man a heart attack, why don't you! Why are you wearing a Halloween costume?"

"It's for medical reasons."

Einstein and the herd had quickly figured out that if they told people that the cloaks were for religious or medical purposes, they were usually left alone. As predicted, Billy grunted and let it slide. He held up his toolbox. "I came prepared." He also held up the beer. "I came really prepared. What're we working on?"

Einstein took a few stiff steps out of the house, shutting the door behind him with his mind. He stumbled down the porch steps, but with a little telekinesis, managed to stay upright.

Billy followed, watching him carefully. "You sure you don't want to take that sheet off your head? It ain't going to rain."

"Thank you," Einstein huffed, moving toward the barn, "but I am deathly allergic to sunlight."

"Suit yourself," Billy said with a shrug.

They entered the barn. Surprise overtook the old man's face once again as he observed the scattered pieces of the laser littering the ground. "What is all this?"

Einstein's mind went blank. "A laser." He was never good at making up stories.

"Now listen here," said Billy, backing away. "I don't want no trouble. If this is gonna be used in some scheme, I want no part in it."

"It's not part of a scheme," Einstein protested. "It's, uh... to help me return."

"What?" said Billy, his brow creasing.

Einstein hobbled to the middle of the floor, careful not to crush any laser parts. He lifted a few small pieces with his mind and juggled them. "It's to help me return," Einstein insisted again. "I'm not from here, and I'm very homesick."

Billy's jaw dropped. He attempted to speak a few

times, but shook his head, watching the laser pieces spin around and around in the air. Finally, a grin spread over his entire face, and he let out a barely audible, "I knew it."

What he knew, Einstein wasn't sure, but he wasn't about to pry. "Can you help me?"

"Of course," said Billy. "Where do we start?"

They set about studying the blueprints. Einstein located the correct parts and sent them floating Billy's way, and Billy put them together. At first they worked in silence, struggling to make sense of the design. But as they fell into a rhythm, Einstein caught Billy stealing glances at him. They assembled the barrel, then the tripod. As Billy attached them, he looked over his shoulder at Einstein again.

"What's up?" he asked.

"I've wanted to meet one of you ever since I was a little kid," Billy said, fastening the bolts of the tripod to the barrel.

"One of me?" Einstein said in confusion.

"A space alien. I saw one in the woods behind my parents' house. No one ever believed me."

"I'm sorry to hear that."

"Could you sit this up? I don't wanna throw out my back," Billy asked, indicating the tripod.

"Sure thing." Einstein closed his eyes and pulled the apparatus to a standing position with his mind. He gulped in a deep breath of air. The laser was getting heavier.

"Does that hurt?"

"It's exhausting, and I'm out of practice," said the llama.

"Could I learn?"

"We really need to finish this first."

They continued to piece the laser together until at last it was finished. Billy paced, examining it. The contraption came up to his shoulders and looked like something out of a comic book. The barrel of the laser had a gaping hole, where Einstein assumed the power source belonged. It also had a seat that could swivel with the laser, and a panel with a big, red button. "How are you making it run?"

"A power source is being brought as we speak."

When Einstein didn't elaborate, Billy nodded. "This thing is safe, right? It won't blow up the barn or nothin'?"

Einstein didn't have an answer. He studied the blueprints again. The ray would be powerful, but he wasn't sure how much use it would be on the ground. He stared at the ceiling, trying to think of a place to set it up to maximize efficiency. "The roof," he said. "Yes, that's it! The roof will give us the best vantage point."

"What's that?" said Billy, cupping a hand to his ear.

"I want to lift it to the roof. Uhh... that way it doesn't vaporize me," Einstein said louder.

Billy laughed. "You're on your own there! I couldn't lift this thing if I tried, and I'm not taking it apart."

Einstein drew in a deep breath. "I think I can do it. Stand back."

Billy retreated against the wall as Einstein left the walker behind and planted all four hooves on the ground. Making sure the cloak still covered him, he turned his attention on the laser, mentally sizing it up.

First, he needed it out of the barn. Filling his lungs again, he closed his eyes and *willed* it to move. In an instant, energy drained from Einstein's body, and he was left panting. Billy's sharp whistle caused him to open his eyes again. Deep scratches in the barn floor led out the door, and the back of the laser glinted under the sunlight.

"That was mighty impressive," said Billy, genuine awe in his voice. "Are you okay?"

"Yes!" Einstein laughed with exhilaration at his feat. He ran out the door, situated himself in front of the laser again, closed his eyes, and sent out another burst of psychic energy. His brain throbbed, as if it were about to explode, but he didn't relent. Cracking one eye, he saw the contraption wobbling a few feet off the ground.

"Careful now, don't hurt yourself," Billy said, voice tight with worry.

But Einstein continued to push himself, and the

laser continued to rise. At last, the feet of the tripod touched the surface of the roof. He released his grip as Billy gave a wild, "WHOOP!" and became caught in a fit of exhilarated laughter.

Einstein's legs wobbled, and he collapsed where he stood.

"Whoah, whoah!" Billy cried, running forward to help him. Einstein's hood fell back from his head, and the old man gasped.

"A llama?"

He reached forward a tentative hand, as if to touch Einstein's snout, but quickly withdrew it. "You're mimicking one of Elsie's llamas. That's amazing."

Einstein weakly nudged his arm. "I think I've overworked myself."

"Is there anything you need?" Billy asked, his expression, serious. "I don't know what sorts of food that beings such as yourself eat, but I have some leftovers in my fridge at home, and I always keep those little chocolate and peanut butter candies around in case of situations like this."

Einstein wagged his tail. "I think some hay and water will suffice. But afterward, I will need to sleep." He touched his nose to the man's arm again in gratitude. "I must ask you to stay inside for the rest of today and tonight. I'm afraid that if my friends see you when they come to retrieve me, they won't understand."

Billy's shoulders slumped a little, but he nodded. "Will I ever see you again, friend?"

Einstein flicked his ears. "Perhaps. Who knows what the future will bring."

Billy finally worked up the courage to pat his nose, then stood and left to find hay. Einstein laid his head on the ground in complete exhaustion, glad he could finally drop his character. His muscles shook and his head felt as if it would implode. If the Eels arrived within the next hour, he doubted he would wake up for them. He fell asleep before Billy returned with the food and water.

22: Strategy

GRETCHEN TRIED six times to properly park the car and trailer in an unobtrusive spot in front of the supermarket. In the end, she left it to take up two and a half spaces, as she planned on being quick anyway.

"What are we here for?" Melville asked as she locked the car door.

"Bait."

The automatic doors to the store slid open with a hiss, and a rush of cold air escaped. Gretchen took a cart, her feet turning toward the meat section. Plastic-wrapped tubs of bright red meat lined the shelves. Beef, turkey, pork—hopefully, all tantalizing options for a giant, toothy alien. She sought out the least expensive of the selection and piled them into her cart as quickly as she could.

A man standing in front of the steaks raised an

eyebrow at her and she returned a sheepish smile. "I'm having a party tonight."

"Can I come?" he chuckled.

"Trust me, you don't want to."

Gretchen piled the meat in until the cart was full and then wheeled toward the checkout line, drawing a few curious stares. The monotonous beeps of scanners rang out at each station as she joined the shortest line. She rested her elbows on her cart handle. Another customer stepped in behind her.

"Gretchen! I've been looking for you all day."

Her stomach sank at the familiar voice. "Hi, Priscilla."

Gretchen turned to find her cousin holding a gallon of milk and wearing a forced smile. Priscilla side-eyed her cart, but made no comment on it. "Did you talk to Penelope yet?" Her calm, even voice was so different from the last time they'd talked. There was something... off putting about it.

Gretchen laughed nervously. "Not yet."

Though the line hadn't moved, she took another step toward the cashier. But the cart was heavy, and she misjudged the amount of force necessary to move it. It careened to the side and would've collided with the candy display had not Priscilla's hand shot out and grabbed it.

"Thanks," Gretchen said.

Priscilla didn't let go. In fact, her grip tightened,

fingers twining through the metal bars. "What's the holdup?" she asked, her voice keeping its sweet tone despite the iciness of her expression. "I thought you were ready to be rid of it."

Gretchen shrugged. "I might've been wrong."

She blinked, and the facade cracked a little. "Excuse me?"

"I... uh... don't think I should sell it to you."

"Excuse me?"

Priscilla pulled the basket toward her with surprising strength and Gretchen instinctively stepped back a couple of paces. "Not you specifically! I don't think I should sell it to anyone!"

Priscilla advanced, her wide eyes and scowl causing her to look unhinged. "No!" she snarled, voice rising with each word. "You said I could have it! That farm was promised to me, and you can't take it away!"

"How about we talk about this next week?" Gretchen said, keeping her own tone calm and even.

"I can't fathom why Elsie left it to you," Priscilla sneered, accusation heavy in her tone. "You don't belong on a farm. You're going to destroy it. I came by this morning and the door was hanging open, no one was home, and one of the llamas was pacing around the kitchen! You're careless! Not fit to run the place! I saw your little science experiment and how you're treating those llamas! Elsie would've been ashamed of you!"

At those words, something snapped in Gretchen. She balled her fists and steeled her composure. "Elsie chose me," she said, then gently pried the shopping cart away from her cousin and moved to greet the cashier. The woman looked concerned at the amount of meat, but didn't say anything as she scanned the items. Out of the corner of her eye, Gretchen saw Priscilla push through a group of people and bolt out the door. She supposed she'd have to deal with her later. But for now...

Everything else could wait.

Hildegard Farm was at stake.

She handed her credit card to the cashier, trying not to think too hard about the price on the checkout screen, and helped load the shopping bags into the cart.

Pushing her purchases back to her car, she emptied it into the back seat under the uneasy eyes of the herd, returned the shopping cart, and left the store behind.

THE SUN SANK FURTHER and further toward the earth. It bathed the landscape in its fiery orange glow for only a fleeting handful of moments before plunging below the horizon and cloaking the world in darkness. By the time Gretchen parked outside Elsie's house, the sky had faded into an inky black expanse, and as she stared up at it, she felt terribly, terribly small.

She took a moment to rest her shaking forearms against the steering wheel. The confidence she'd felt at the arcade was beginning to ebb, and all she could think of were the teeth. Big. Sharp. Pointed.

She jumped when Einstein's nose suddenly appeared at the window. He excitedly nodded in greeting, causing an odd-looking helmet on his head to slip over his eyes. "Come on! We don't have long," he said in a hoarse voice.

Gretchen clambered out of the car, then picked up Neel. The herd, including Melville, gathered around her and stood to attention.

"What's the first order of business?" Austen asked.

Gretchen stood as tall and straight as she could. "We need to set a trap. To lure the Eels in so we can zap them. I have what I hope will do the trick in the car, but everything that comes after luring them will depend entirely on our ability to work together. Understood?"

Llama heads bobbed in agreement.

She turned to Einstein. "Did you figure out what telekinesis the documents were referring to?"

Einstein's entire body perked up, and he wiggled his ears.

"I think he did," laughed Shelley.

"What are you wearing?" asked Verne.

But Einstein ignored them as he waggled his tail and edged back from the group. "Come and see!"

They set off in the direction of the barn, and Gretchen noticed a slight limp in Einstein's gait.

"Are you okay?" she asked.

"Of course! More than okay! Look up there!" he said, pointing with his nose to the roof, where the completed shrink ray stood silhouetted against the night sky. His chest swelled with pride.

"I know you're smart, but how the heck did you get that up there?" Gretchen said. "And, uh... What's on your head?"

"Don't worry about it," he replied, nudging her toward the barn. "Go on and put the power source in!"

Gretchen walked around the barn until she found a ladder leaning against its side. She triple checked that its feet were firmly planted on the ground, then climbed to the roof. The laser seemed even bigger up close. She withdrew the glowing green cylinder from her messenger bag, and after a bit of searching, found a perfectly cylindrical compartment to slide it into. As soon as she did so, the entire apparatus hummed and grew warm.

"Bring something for me to test this on!" she called.

Twain disappeared into the barn and then reappeared, pushing a lawn chair across the ground with his head.

"Perfect! Now stand back!"

The llamas retreated to a safe distance. Gretchen felt like she was playing an arcade game as she aimed and pressed a red button on the joystick. A blazing green beam shot out from the end of the apparatus and hit the chair.

At first, nothing happened.

But then...

The chair shrank.

Giddiness overtook Gretchen as she descended the ladder. The miniature lawn chair lay on its side in the grass, where it had been hit. She stooped to pick it up and examined its delicate legs and tiny, striped seat with awe. It could've been made for a doll house.

Gretchen eyed the laser and then the area surrounding her and walked away from the barn, carefully measuring each stride.

"What are you thinking?" Shelley asked.

Gretchen continued until she reached the edge of the ditch where she'd found Neel's egg. "I want to set the trap here."

"Of course," said Twain, following. "We'll do whatever you ask of us."

She took in the mud and water below. "This is the perfect spot to lay a feast for our visitors."

Einstein's eyes widened as he connected the dots. "Draw them to one place, and then attack!"

"Exactly!" she said. "And hopefully all the commotion will draw the Queen."

A shudder ran through the herd, but it was accompanied by solemn nods.

"Let's get to work."

Gretchen took Neel into the farmhouse and locked him in her room. She didn't want him getting mixed up in the battle. She then went to the garage and gathered as many supplies as she could into the cart that the llamas had pulled her in the first night she'd known them. Then, wheeling the cart to the barn, she and the herd began to carry out their plan.

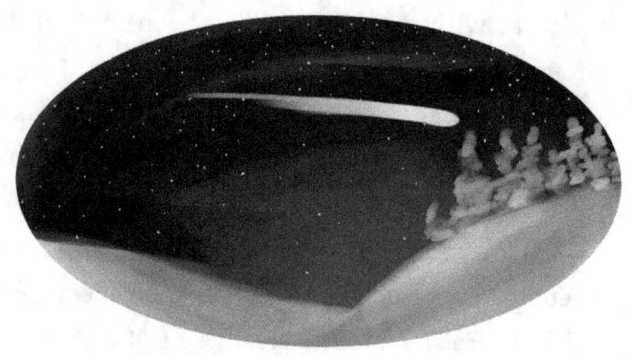

23: Arrival

Deep in the ditch, which Gretchen and the herd had come to refer to as the Pit, Shelley and Gretchen tipped over the first of two large buckets of meat. They decided to set one out at a time so that it wouldn't all be eaten at once, and to store the other in the barn until it was needed. It wouldn't last long, but Gretchen hoped that once one Eel came to investigate the smell, the others would follow.

"This is nasty," the llama said as the last bits of ground beef plopped into the mud below. Her eyes flashed green as she turned her head.

Gretchen sank to her knees and pressed a hand into the cold, slimy chunk, spreading it as best she could. "Agreed."

They'd picked the driest part of the ditch, though a shallow pool of water still covered the bottom. The meat had been spread over outcroppings above the water line. Gretchen was glad she couldn't see the awful mixture very well in the dark.

Above them, Brontë, Austen, and Twain finished erecting a set of mist nets, typically used for catching songbirds, which they'd found in the garage. They planned on chasing smaller Eels into it if necessary. On the other side of the Pit, closer to the barn, Verne and Einstein practiced operating a couple of flood-lights, hooked up to an old generator that surprisingly still ran. Gretchen could hear them banter as they worked.

"No, no, no," said Verne. "An Eel wouldn't do it like that. Try it like this." The dazzling light blinked on and off in a choppy pattern.

"That's not right, either," huffed Einstein.

When Gretchen was satisfied with the spread of bait, she stood and shook her hands off, sending bits of meat flying. She poked her head up from the Pit and observed their hard work. "It's definitely crazy," she admitted to herself. "But what else can we do?"

The floodlights shone again, and she spotted Melville near the barn, vigilantly staring up at the sky.

"See anything?" she called.

"Not a monster in sight! Are you sure you read the radar right?" he asked Einstein.

"Positive," Einstein said.

A sudden plopping sound caused Gretchen to turn

her attention back to the Pit. "Hey Shelley, we're only setting out the one bucket, remember?"

"That's not me," Shelley said.

The ominous plopping continued, growing louder and faster. Gretchen squinted into the darkness and gasped at the approach of a hoard of shimmering elvers, just below the surface of the murky water. "NO!" she shouted as they broke free from the water and descended on the bait, squealing and snapping. "They'll eat everything before the big ones get here!" Mud caked her shoes as she slid to the bottom.

"Here!" Shelley called, kicking the empty bucket down as well.

Gretchen grabbed it and scooped up several hungry little fiends. She slipped out of her hoodie and used it to cover the top, but instantly regretted the decision. The ones she hadn't caught nipped at her exposed skin as she continued to snatch elver after elver and shove them into the bucket. But there were too many.

"Aren't you going to help?!" she snarled up at the llamas, who had gathered around the Pit to watch. She must've sounded fierce, because the elvers stopped their wild frenzy and hung in the air as if dazed.

"Ha!" she said, triumphantly picking up the closest. She reached for the next, but a pit deeper than the one she was standing in formed in her stomach. Something was wrong.

A gasp went up among the herd, and they turned their gazes upward. The elvers in the bucket stopped struggling, and the rest fled. Gretchen climbed up the side of the Pit and propped an elbow on the edge to steady herself.

They appeared between the scintillating stars—tiny pinpricks of light in the night sky. But as they drew closer, those pinpricks elongated until their snaking undulations became visible. Gretchen tensed as anxious hums sounded among the llamas. Shelley's ears flicked back against her head, and she said in her low voice, "Here they come."

Gretchen climbed the rest of the way out of the Pit and brushed herself off. "Everyone to their stations. Stick to the plan, and we will be fine."

The llamas dispersed. Brontë, Austen, and Twain resumed their guard by the nets, and Verne took up his place by the lights. Gretchen, Einstein, and Melville retreated to the barn. Once inside, Gretchen put her bucket of elvers on the ground, upside down, and placed a stray brick on top. She then turned to the cart she'd brought over from the garage.

The floodlight outside flickered its signal as Gretchen equipped herself. The grappling hook and rope, she wound over her shoulders, like a sash. She clipped two blasters from the box Einstein brought from the lab, one at each hip, to her belt and gripped a third in her hand. She'd laughed when she'd first seen them—they looked exactly like the ones at the arcade. But when she pulled the trigger, the thing emitted a dangerous whine that caused her to immediately let go. Beside her, Einstein telekinetically picked up the rest of the blasters. They hovered around him, whining in the same manner as they hummed to life.

"Don't overdo it," she said.

He nodded and trotted back out to join Verne.

Gretchen turned back to the cart and picked out an empty jar with a bit of rope tied around the top to hold it. She slipped the rope over her shoulder alongside the grappling hook.

"What's that for?" asked Melville.

"We need something to hold the shrunken Eels," she said, beckoning him to follow her to the barn door. She powered up the blaster in her hand.

"I hope you know what you're doing," he said, gazing up at the Eels.

Uncertainty churned in Gretchen's belly, but she nodded. They parted ways—Melville joining the net team as Gretchen climbed the ladder to the roof. She clambered into the laser's seat, feeling the entire apparatus vibrate around her. Sighting down the barrel, she aimed at the Eels and waited. "Here they come."

The former pinpricks kept stretching until they became long ribbons, lazily drifting in the atmosphere. Gretchen counted five. They were enormous and stunningly beautiful. The coiled carcass she'd seen the other day didn't do the species justice.

Below, Verne redoubled his light-flickering, and Gretchen felt a twisted sense of relief as the wave of Eels curiously drifted closer. Then, all at once, as if they hit an invisible wall over the Pit, they took a downward turn and fell like rain in slow-motion. It reminded Gretchen of the glittering trails left by fireworks. Goosebumps rose along her arms, and she suddenly found it hard to swallow.

One Eel sped up and arrived at one of the meat piles before the others. Gretchen took aim at it and mashed the red button on the laser's joystick.

BZZZZZZT!

The entire laser recoiled as it sent out a narrow beam, which cut through the air and hit the Eel square on its nose. The creature shrieked in anger, altering its trajectory to head straight for Gretchen. She tensed, bracing herself for the inevitable impact, but right as the thing opened its great jaws, it began to shrink.

The Eel careened to its side and desperately thrashed as it grew smaller and smaller. When it reached half its original size, Gretchen swiveled the laser and hit it again, this time, holding the red button until the Eel became a tiny dot in the grass.

As the first one fell, the others scattered. The llamas let out a collective war cry and dashed after the fleeing creatures. They broke into pairs, except

Einstein, who stood at the ready with his blasters. Globs of acid spit flew through the air, causing Eels to shriek in pain whenever they were hit and driving them toward Einstein.

As Gretchen sought out the fourth remaining Eel, she was glad that Verne had left the floodlight on. She spotted it, heading toward the retention pond, and made short work of it.

Gretchen descended the ladder with her jar and searched around for the downed Eels. She found one drunkenly zig-zagging in front of the barn. Without thinking, she reached out and cupped her hands around it, as if she were catching a firefly. She brought her hands close and peeked between her thumbs.

The Eel now measured the length of her ring finger. It emitted a soft glow, much like the elvers, but it retained all of the adult features and its glow still pulsed and changed colors in wild, unpredictable patterns. A goofy grin spread over her face as the miniature Eel hissed at her.

"You're adorable! A mini Neel!" she crooned.

Needle-like teeth sank into the fleshy part of her left palm in response.

"AGH!"

Gretchen shook the creature off, into the jar at her hip. She shut the lid with a *snap!* and latched it into place. Blood beaded on her palm, so she wiped it on her jeans.

"We got them!" called Twain as Gretchen jogged over to join him. Three tiny Eels squirmed in the mesh of the net.

"That was awesome!" Shelley laughed. "We chased them right in!"

She and Austen pranced around each other.

Gretchen took down the poles and untangled the Eels. Two dropped into the jar. The third gave a great squirm and landed in the grass. Gretchen bent to grasp it gently, but firmly behind the head. It wriggled uselessly as she brought it to her side, and into the jar it went.

"Here, help me with this," she said, indicating the net.

Einstein telekinetically assisted her in resetting the poles. Once they were jammed firmly back in the ground, Melville bounded toward the group from the other side of the barn. "Gretchen!" he called.

"Look! It's working!" she said, holding up her glowing jar with pride. The Eels sulked inside.

Melville spared them the smallest of glances. "Yes, but not fast enough. A new wave dropped in on the north side of the property and is headed this way."

Gretchen and the other llamas gathered around him and searched the sky until they spotted the slowly waving ribbons of light, descending toward the Earth.

24: Invasion

THE SECOND ATTACK found the inhabitants of Hildegard Farm prepared. Verne and Einstein flashed their floodlight, drawing the fresh wave of Eels toward the Pit, and Gretchen trained her laser on them. As the Eels approached the light, they matched its pattern with their own blinking bioluminescence.

"Eighteen, nineteen, twenty," Gretchen counted under her breath. She let out a low whistle. "Four times the size of the last wave."

She watched as Shelley, Austen, Brontë, Twain, and Melville ran out to meet them, sending globs of acid spit hurtling into the sky. The globs that hit their marks sent Eels madly wriggling away from the band of ungulates. Gretchen waited until a few seemed closer and set her sights on the nearest one. She smashed the red button with her thumb and sent several beams at the creatures, but the shots fell short. The Eels were out of range.

Gretchen stood in her chair and wildly waved her arms at the herd. "Chase them closer!" she yelled, but nobody seemed to hear her. She plopped back into the seat and eyed an Eel through the scope. The laser hummed and shook as it powered up, but this time, Gretchen pressed the button and held it down for a longer time. An odd whine emanated from somewhere inside. "No, no, no!" she yelled as its humming slowed and the power began to fail. "You've got to be kidding me!"

She removed the power source and found that the once green glowing substance within had been completely drained. With a hiss, she jumped to her feet and slid down the ladder to the ground, and, unholstering one of her blasters, she dashed toward the fray.

A cacophony of shrieks and hums met her ears as she drew closer to the chaos. The arcade replicas didn't do justice to the sheer size and prowess of the Eels. They swooped low, some snapping at the herd, while others began nuzzling at the ground, scraping away large clumps of earth with their noses. Up ahead, one bore down on Austen with jaws parted wide. Gretchen raised her blaster, aimed, and shrank it before its teeth could close on the llama.

"Thanks!" Austen panted as Gretchen collected the

Eel. She observed the burrowing Eels. "What's going on? Why are they doing that?"

"I think they're nesting," said Gretchen.

Not far from them, Twain led another Eel toward Einstein and his eerily floating blasters. Beams of light shot forth, and the tiny monster fell to the grass. The Eel rose into the air again, wriggling and trying to find its bearings. Gretchen leapt on it before it could get away. Her hands wrapped around its lithe body, but it proved to be slippery, and pried itself from her grasp several times. Finally, she pounced, cupped it between both hands, and deposited it into her jar.

"Gretchen! Move!" came Twain's panicked cry from some distance away.

She looked up in time to see a huge Eel, speeding toward her with rage, blazing in its eyes. Gretchen threw herself out of the way just in time. The creature slammed into the ground, throwing up dirt and debris, and leaving a long, ugly scar across the earth. Gretchen pushed herself up on her elbows and squinted, wondering if it was dead. But it gave a great heave and pulled itself out of the hole it had made. It shook the dirt from its snout and flew forth with renewed rage.

Gretchen scratched her arm against something sharp in the grass as she aimed her blaster and sent a couple of beams at the Eel. She let out a breath of relief as she stood, brushed herself off, and bent to pick up the small creature.

Melville skidded to a halt beside her, a horrified expression on his face. "What are you doing here?! You're supposed to be on the roof!"

"The laser quit working!" she shrugged.

His ears flicked back against his head and his eyes flashed. "Then get it to work again!"

At that moment, Einstein galloped toward them. "Another wave is approaching!"

Gretchen wiped a trickle of blood from her arm and let out a tired groan. "How many? How big?"

"About the same as this one."

She swore. "How much meat do we have left?"

"Not much, but if any more waves come, hopefully they see their conspecifics and decide to join the party in the Pit."

"Gretchen!" Brontë called from the direction of the barn. "We need you over here!"

"Coming!"

"Gretchen, get back on the roof and fix the laser!" Melville protested.

She ruffled the top of his head and took off.

Brontë met her beside the barn. "We're having trouble getting the net up again," she said. "The poles keep falling over."

Gretchen peered around her to see Shelley and Austen struggling to push the net upright again. In the Pit below, Twain emptied the last bucket of meat. She cringed at the pitiful offering, hoping it would be enough to attract at least a few more Eels. The shimmering in the north grew steadily closer. Gretchen approached Shelley and Austen.

"Need a hand?"

"Opposable thumbs would be nice," said Shelley.

Gretchen slid in beside them and pushed the first pole up. The soft earth around it did nothing to offer support, so she stamped it in with her shoe. When she was satisfied it wouldn't fall over, she moved to the next.

"I don't know if we will be able to fight them all," said Shelley. "I'm so tired already." Shivers ran through her legs, and the white parts of her eyes shone in the floodlight.

Gretchen pushed the second pole into place and the net billowed out. "Hang in there," she said.

Melville appeared at her elbow and helped squish the soil around the pole's base. "We're all tired," he snapped.

Einstein returned to the group, a shrunken Eel squirming in his telekinetic grasp.

"YEAH!" Gretchen yelled, punching the air with her fist. She was surprised he still had energy, but he laughed as he dropped his prisoner into the jar. She held a hand out and he bopped it with his nose.

The moment was short-lived.

A fiery glow on the horizon drew their attention.

"Holy—" Gretchen breathed.

Three more waves of Eels rained from the heavens. "There are too many," Melville said. "We can't take them all at once."

Gretchen met his eyes. "We also can't back out now."

They grouped in front of the barn and resumed their stations as the next wave arrived. Verne fervently flashed the floodlight, beckoning the Eels toward them. Gretchen tried to count them as they arrived, but quickly became overwhelmed. Most began burrowing into the ground as soon as they arrived, but a few came to check out the lights and smells of the Pit. As the curious Eels swarmed the last of the food, Gretchen set her sights on the largest individual. But as she took aim, it noticed her. It swerved around the shots in mid-air and headed away from the Pit.

"Oh no you don't!" she called, sliding the rope and grappling hook from her shoulder. She swung it a few times, aimed, and hurled it as hard as she could. It sailed through the air and hooked around a dorsal spike. Gretchen dug her heels into the soft earth, pulling back toward the pit, but the Eel was stronger. With a fierce flail, it knocked Gretchen to the ground and dragged her toward the woods. Gretchen held on for dear life as the Eel bucked and twisted in futile attempts to free itself of the grappling hook. It wasn't until they were in the woods that it broke free. It slammed against the trunk of a large oak, knocking the grappling hook to the ground.

Without thinking, Gretchen stood and leaned against another tree, panting. The Eel's attention snapped to her. "Oh boy," she breathed. She turned and pelted through the woods as fast as she could.

As Gretchen dodged between trees, the Eel slid through them with ease, its bioluminescence throwing their bark into sharp relief as it passed. She frantically glanced over her shoulder and a raised root snagged her foot, sending her sprawling into a ditch. Water soaked her skin and clothes, and her glasses landed somewhere in the leaf litter. Coughing and spluttering, she twisted around, instinctively reaching to find them, and her heart nearly stopped. The blurry form of the Eel loomed over her, mouth open, sharp teeth gleaming in its own glow. It reared back in preparation to strike. She reached for her blaster, only to find it gone.

Pew! Pew!

Bright green lasers cut the night, shooting from a blaster as it thumped against the ground. The lasers hit the creature between the eyes, and it let out a horrible shriek as it shrank and plopped into the water. Melville panted at the edge of the ditch, from where he'd kicked the blaster.

"Are you alright?" he called.

"Yeah. Thanks," said Gretchen, moving toward the bright speck in the water.

"No problem," said Melville.

She scooped the angry Eel in her jar with one hand. Beneath the surface, something long and slimy slid past Gretchen's propped arm. She recoiled with a shout.

"What?" Melville cried, his dark shape dancing anxiously in place.

Gretchen plunged a hand underwater and drew out a long, snake-like creature. She squinted at its dull body and smiled when she spotted the tiny limbs. "It's an amphiuma!"

"Gretchen, this is no time for herpetology!"

A burst of light from overhead startled them both, and the amphiuma fell back into the water with a splash. Through a break in the foliage above, Gretchen and Melville watched as the largest Eel yet flew past. It was easily ten times the size of the one that had dragged Getchen through the woods. Its lateral spots burned like fiery eyes, blinking down at them, and it slid through the sky at a leisurely pace, as if it expected the universe to be waiting on it. Unhurried. Regal. "The Queen," Gretchen whispered.

"We have to get back," Melville said, his voice trembling slightly.

They took off in the direction of the barn, running as fast as they could.

25: CRISIS

EERIE SILENCE HUNG over the world when Gretchen and Melville broke through the woods and crossed back into the field in front of the Pit. They came upon a lone Eel, snuffling the dirt in search of any remnants of meat, but it paid them no attention. Gretchen's heart beat in her throat as she surveyed the area, however, the rest of the herd and the other Eels were nowhere in sight. The fields beyond the barn were dark and still. Lifeless. *Empty.* Gretchen felt Melville shiver beside her, and her own blood felt icy in her veins.

"Where are they?" he whispered.

She didn't know how to answer, so she took off running toward the barn. The floodlight lay where it had fallen on its side, casting its beam of white light across the ground.

"Gretchen!"

Melville's hoofsteps drummed against the ground

behind her, but she didn't slow until she reached the wooden side of the building. The llama skidded to a halt beside her, wide eyes glowing in the darkness.

"Gretchen, they can't be dead," he said. "They're my brothers. My sisters."

She leaned against the barn, panting. "We don't know what's going on, okay? They're fine."

At a loss for what to do, she paced, pulling at her hair in distress. How could they all just be *gone?*

A brief flash in the distance caught her eye. When it came again, she could see it came from the window of the farmhouse. Beckoning Melville to follow, she started toward it.

The door to the farmhouse hung open. Gretchen gripped her blaster as she carefully peered into the shadowy interior. Whatever had been glowing had disappeared. "Hello?" she called in a low voice. "Einstein? Shelley?"

"Don't go in," Melville said.

Gretchen patted him on the neck and stepped inside. The floorboards creaked treacherously underfoot. It looked as if something large had come through. The couches were skewed and one of the bookshelves had been knocked over, leaving a pile of books strewn across the floor.

"They're obviously not here," he hissed.

Gretchen bent, picked up a book, and dusted off its cover, which glinted in the soft glow of her jar. It was one of her study guides. She ran her thumb over the title. That part of her life felt so far away. Clutching the book to her chest, she cast another glance about the room, searching for any clue as to the fate of the herd. But she found nothing.

"Let's go," Melville urged.

"Okay," she said.

But before she could move, Melville froze, ears twitching. "Do you hear that?"

"Hear what?" she asked.

All at once, an Eel coiled against the ceiling lit the room like an oversized firefly. Gretchen and Melville gave shouts of surprise and dove out of the way as it struck. It turned and snapped at Gretchen, and she reflexively hurled her textbook at it. With a second snap, it swallowed the book whole.

"Shoot it!" Melville yelled.

Gretchen raised her blaster and sent a beam at it. The Eel shrank, but not quite enough. It was still the length of both Gretchen's arms as it attacked again. It wrapped itself around her torso and sank its teeth into her shoulder. Searing pain ripped across her muscles as she frantically tried to peel her attacker off. Melville leaned in to bite it, but at the same moment, Gretchen's elbow collided with his snout as she flailed her arm.

"HELP!" she screamed as the Eel constricted her.

A fiery comet streaked across the room. She tried

to scream again, but the Eel was squeezing so tightly that she had a hard time drawing in air.

But then, the pressure lifted, and the teeth pulled out of her shoulder. Gretchen sucked in a deep breath as an ear-splitting shriek emanated from the Eel. The fiery comet attacked again, so fast that Gretchen could hardly register what was happening, but she was able to catch a glimpse when it finally began to slow. Her mouth fell open. It was Neel. He sunk his teeth into the other Eel, just behind its head, and wrapped himself around its writhing body, bullying it further and further away from Gretchen. The other Eel somehow managed to wriggle free, but Neel continued to drive it into the kitchen. He caught it by the head again and flung it against the wall, and the creature fell to the floor, stunned.

Gretchen pressed a hand to her shoulder in an attempt to staunch the blood seeping from it, and approached the downed Eel. It lay limp where it had fallen, but she could still see its nostrils flaring with rage. Neel nipped at its tail as she picked it up.

"Good boy," she said hoarsely.

"I didn't think he had it in him," Melville said, looking on in bewilderment.

A sudden desire to get out of the house over-whelmed Gretchen, and she pushed open the door to the back porch and stepped outside, still clutching the unconscious Eel in her hand. Melville followed at her heels.

"Is there anywhere the herd would've run to?" she asked.

"I don't know," Melville said. When he looked at Gretchen, tears welled in his eyes. "I've never been apart from them. Things have been so hard since Elsie died, but at least we had each other."

Gretchen nodded.

"Then you came along," he said. "I was skeptical. You were supposed to replace Elsie, but... No one can ever replace her."

"They can't," Gretchen said. "I'm sorry that I never got to know her."

"You remind me a lot of her. You even look a little like her." He fell quiet and resumed scanning the darkness. Gretchen wondered how well he could see through it.

The Eel in her hand suddenly came to. It twisted itself out of her grasp and rose into the air, its attention riveted on something in the distance. With a shout, Gretchen tried to catch it, but the creature flew out of reach. As if following an invisible trail, it slithered forward through the air.

Other, larger Eels faded into view, all moving in the same direction and in the same slow, intent manner. Neel slid past Gretchen's ear, and she shot out her hand and caught him before he could get away. He struggled in her hands.

"What's gotten into you?" she grunted, pinning him under her arm.

Green light bathed the landscape, pulling her attention away from her pet. The light faded, then blazed again—this time, pink. The light continued to alternate, its rhythm like a heartbeat.

"It's her," Melville breathed.

In the distance, the Queen descended from the sky. Hundreds of Eels had made their way into the hills and fields, and they all altered their light patterns to match hers. Elvers popped out of the grass and wriggled away in droves. One hill became silhouetted in the glow, and the Queen circled it, snipping lazily at the approaching Eels. Those that reached it, began to burrow.

Neel became more desperate in his attempts to escape and join the droves. Gretchen wrestled him back inside, and for lack of a better idea, shoved him into the refrigerator and shut the door. "I'll come back for you!"

Outside, she found Melville frantically pacing, eyes glued to the sea of monsters before him. "They're out there. They're out there among those *things*," Melville stammered. "I just know it. I have to find them."

Gretchen opened her mouth to respond, but a terrified scream split the air. It came from the hill.

They exchanged glances and took off running in the direction of the sound. More terrified screams rose, presumably from a hole where their friends were trapped. What happened next drew a fresh wave of horror. Eels, seemingly fascinated by the screams, swarmed the hill, burrowing into it from all angles.

"What do we do?" sobbed Melville. "They're going to be eaten."

Numbness overtook Gretchen's body. "I don't know."

She watched their long bodies, twisting elegantly as they scraped and carved at the dirt with their snouts, their lures and spots bobbing with a hypnotic sort of grace. It wasn't fair that they were so deadly.

"We need help," Gretchen said, tearing her gaze away.

"But who would help us?" Melville asked with a sniff.

Without answering, Gretchen took off toward the house. She couldn't recall ever running so fast. By the time she reached the door, her muscles screamed for relief and her breath came in gasps. Melville barreled into her, knocking her off her feet. The jar of Eels clunked against the wooden boards of the porch, but to her relief, the lid stayed shut and glass didn't scuff.

Gretchen pushed herself back up and twisted the door handle. She tossed a wild glance around the dark room, trying to orient herself as she located the phone.

It hung on the wall in the kitchen, and she yanked it off its receiver and dialed 9-1-1 with trembling fingers. A low dial tone sounded. Melville hovered at her side, the whites of his freakishly green eyes visible in the darkness.

"9-1-1. What's your emergency?" came the cool voice of the first responder.

Gretchen wiped her eyes and pushed past the lump in her throat. "I need help! We're under attack and I don't know what to do!"

"Ma'am, can you tell me where you are? Who's attacking?"

A loud crash outside caused Gretchen and Melville to startle.

"Are you there?"

"I'm at Hill Farm!" Gretchen yelled into the phone.

"What?"

"Hill Farm! Happy - Iguana - Lizard - Lionfish, Farm!"

"I don't think those are the correct codes," said Melville.

"Ma'am, what's your emergency?"

"Aliens are attacking my farm!" she yelled into the phone. "I need backup, now!"

"Ma'am... Is this a joke?"

Gretchen slammed the phone into the receiver in frustration. *Help wasn't coming.*

Melville had become hysterical. "Elsie!" he cried. "I need Elsie!"

Gretchen took a step toward him and slipped on a book. She picked it up. One of Elsie's journals. The glow from her jar lit her great aunt's drawing of the looming Eel, lightning emanating from its lure. Her hand strayed to her blaster in its holster. The trigger wiggled beneath her finger as she ran her eyes over Elsie's handwriting. "Boosts the signal," she murmured. *What if...*

Melville's eyes were now glued to the window, and he let out several big sniffs. "Let's get out of here. I—I don't think I can bear to watch this anymore," he said in a broken voice.

"We're not going anywhere," Gretchen said, pushing past him. She shouldered her way through the door, leapt down the porch steps, and hit the ground running. She raced toward the fray with Melville hot on her heels.

"Wait!" he panted. "Come back!"

She ignored him.

"Please! Don't leave me alone!"

She reached the foot of the hill.

"Elsie, I can't lose you, too!" Melville cried, snatching the edge of her shirt.

His eyes widened as he realized the shirt belonged to Gretchen, but still he didn't let go.

"I know what I'm doing!" she yelled, wrenching her shirt from his teeth. "You have to trust me!"

His reply was lost in the terrified bleats of the other llamas as she pelted across the field and up the hill. The great form of the Queen Eel loomed before her, bent and fixated on a large hole in the ground. It looked as if an Eel had started and abandoned a burrow. The cries of her friends came from within.

"HEY!" Gretchen yelled.

The earth shimmered beneath her feet.

Blazing pink eyes turned on her.

"Leave them alone!"

The head ornamentation flared.

Jaws parted.

Gretchen aimed her blaster at its lure and, without skipping a beat, pulled the trigger. She aimed true, and the Eel let out a horrifying screech, the lights along its body flashing with dazzling color as vibrant green waves engulfed the creature. Gretchen kept the beam concentrated on it until its lure, its spots, and even its eyes shone with the green light. The Eel writhed and twisted its body, unable to break free from the laser's effects, and its screech continued to split the air, piercing Gretchen's eardrums until they felt they might burst.

More Eels had taken interest in the scene, and drifted closer. Jaws snapped hungrily, but they seemed unsure about the hideous screeches of the large Eel.

The lure began to pulse, bathing the entire area in the eerie green light. It was steady at first, like a heartbeat, but the flashing increased in frequency until Gretchen felt quite ill and had to squint against it. Then all at once, the flashing ceased, and the Eel went dark. The world was quiet, but only for a moment. A tidal wave of light exploded from the Queen's lure, and Gretchen squeezed her eyes shut and threw an arm over her face.

When it faded enough for her to lower her arm, she looked skyward, and found hundreds of Eels suspended in the air, their fiery stares locked on her...

And they became smaller.

26: Explanations

Tiny Eels rained from the sky and fell to the ground, stunned. Gretchen also collapsed, feeling the firmness of solid earth against her back and the light sensation of grass tickling her skin. Her white-knuckled grip on her blaster caused her hands to ache, but she found that they were too numb to let go of the thing.

Twin beams of yellow light cut through the air, and she jolted upward in panic. Hums of distress came from the llamas as they peeked out of their hole to see a black SUV barrel into view. It skidded to a halt not too far from the group. In a haze, Gretchen couldn't help but wonder how difficult it would be to fix the ruts left by the tires. The front doors sprang open, almost in sync, and Penelope and Edgar clambered out. They sprinted toward Gretchen and stumbled to a halt in front of her, panting.

"Are you alright?" Edgar gasped.

Gretchen nodded, despite the sobs that now shook her body and the hysteria clouding her mind.

"We're so sorry!" Penelope cried. "Our predictions were off and the alerts only came through an hour ago!"

"Are you hurt?" Edgar insisted.

Gretchen's sobs gave way to laughter, and she shakily held up her glowing jar of Eels. Penelope took them from her as Edgar shrugged out of his coat and wrapped it around her shoulders. The llamas, in a similar state of shock, were also laughing, but the Carsens didn't seem to notice. Or if they did, they didn't mind.

Gretchen allowed herself to be led into the back of the SUV. Melville stepped forward, as if to intervene, but Penelope stopped him.

"We'll bring her back. Go get some rest."

Nothing felt real as Gretchen laid across the back seat and shut her eyes. The vehicle bumped and rocked as Penelope drove. She must've drifted off, because the next thing she knew, she was being gently shaken awake. She sat up and rubbed her eyes. They had arrived at a little house on the outskirts of town. The sun peeked over the horizon and threw the soft blue shadows of houses across the street. The sheen of dew bathed the tips of the grass in the yard. The world was quiet.

Edgar helped Gretchen out of the car as Penelope unlocked the front door. Gretchen sleepily took in the house. It was one story and built of brick and gray stone. Neatly trimmed hedges grew in the flower beds, and she was sure she spotted a pair of cat-like eyes flashing beneath one of them.

The lights in the house flicked on and Gretchen tensed. But one of her hosts draped a blanket over her shoulders and she settled. In a haze, she found herself being led into a small dining area beside the kitchen and gently pushed into a chair at the table.

"Coffee or tea?" Penelope asked.

"Coffee would be nice."

Edgar took the seat across from her. "Again, we are both so sorry about tonight. It wasn't supposed to happen like this."

Gretchen propped herself on her elbows. "How was it supposed to happen? You guys pushed the farm on me, but no one told me *anything*."

"The whole team was supposed to be there, and we were supposed to train you. But you said you didn't want the farm, and then we missed the radar, and the herd started acting out—it was a lot going on at once."

Penelope returned with several mugs. She handed one to Gretchen, one to Edgar, and set the third at an empty spot at the table. "Excuse me for a few more minutes. I need to make a call about your jar of Eels."

Gretchen's eyes widened. "Where are they?"

"Don't worry," said Penelope. "I got them out of the car. They're safe. I have a zoologist friend who will want to take a look at them."

She disappeared into another room around the corner before Gretchen could respond. Gretchen turned her attention to the coffee mug. Steam rose from the beverage, and she spent a few moments basking in its warmth before she took a sip. She turned Edgar's excuses over in her mind. "The team?" she said. "Who are you?"

Edgar sighed. "Penelope and I are members of an organization called the Explorers of Earth," he said. "It's an organization for scientists, inventors, mathematicians, artists, *explorers*. We seek knowledge and novelty. We explore the furthest reaches of the Earth. Your great aunt was part of it, too."

"She was a mountaineer," Gretchen said.

Edgar nodded. He opened a photo album and slid it across the table. Photographs of much younger versions of Edgar and Penelope decorated the interior. They were standing beside a small, smiling, wrinkled woman. "She was a kind old woman. She took me and Penelope under her wing when we first joined. She told us all about the invasion that she and her husband witnessed, as well as the one that was coming. We all worked together to try to find a solution."

"And your first thought was to use llamas?"

Edgar laughed. "Not quite! But when funds are limited, you have to work with what you have. Penelope had a connection who ran a llama farm, and we traded some work for a few of his crias—newborn llamas."

"So... Forgive me, but I'm trying to get this story straight..." Gretchen said, leaning back and drumming her fingers against the mug. "*You* were the aliens?"

"No. We're just people. But also, yes," Edgar said. "Years ago, we engineered the llama herd to be able to handle the Eels. We raised them and trained them, encouraging each llama's natural inclinations. Elsie knew the dangers when she bought that farm, and agreed to take Melville and the others in."

"What about the cyclopes?" Gretchen asked.

Puzzlement swept over Edgar's face before realization dawned on him. He laughed. "We were worried about radioactivity. I suppose the hazmat suits did make us seem like one-eyed aliens."

"And you built the laser tag arcade?"

"We needed a way to train the herd. One of our close friends is a sculptor, and he worked from Elsie's drawings to create mechanical versions of the Queen and her brood. We... ah... lost a lot of money doing that, so we decided to sell the pieces to an arcade once we were done with them."

Gretchen frowned. "You didn't think it would be good to keep training with the herd? They didn't feel ready."

Edgar coughed uncomfortably and shifted in his seat. "They weren't. We discontinued the program when we saw they weren't doing well, and they weren't passing any of our tests."

"They did so well out there."

"We misjudged."

An awkward silence followed, and Gretchen flipped through the photo album. The next few pages held images of Edgar and Penelope in various locations—a rocky beach, beneath a giant sequoia tree, on an ice shelf in Antarctica. Her gaze lingered over a photo of a leopard seal, stretched out contentedly on the ice.

"Should you be interested, I'd be happy to introduce you to the current president of the Explorers of Earth," Edgar said quietly.

Gretchen ran her thumb over the photographs. The offer sounded intriguing, but at the same time, it was terrifying. "I..."

She was saved from having to answer as Penelope returned to the room and took a seat beside her husband. "Marla said she would pick up the Eels in the morning. She's very curious to finally see these creatures up close."

"Where are you taking them?" Gretchen asked.

"To a secure location, where we can study them." Penelope took a sip from her coffee mug. "They'll be well taken care of."

"Will I be able to visit them?"

Penelope smiled at her husband in amusement. "My, she's full of questions, isn't she?"

"And she's not too keen on answering mine, I see," Edgar said with a wink. "But that's okay. She's been through a lot tonight. Gretchen, I'll be asking the same question again after you get some rest."

She nodded, feeling like her tongue was suddenly stuck to the roof of her mouth. She lowered her eyes to the photographs again and was surprised to see a wet splotch soaking into the page. Her hand strayed to her face, which flushed with embarrassment when she found the tear tracks.

"I think we should get her home," said Penelope. "The herd probably needs to see that she's alright."

"You're right," said Edgar. They both stood and started bustling around in preparation to leave again. A lump formed in Gretchen's throat as she watched them. As hard as she tried, she could no longer imagine herself being happy in vet school.

"I want to keep the farm," she blurted out.

"Of course," said Penelope.

"What about Priscilla?"

"Gretchen, don't worry. We'll take care of everything."

THE CARSENS DROPPED Gretchen off at the farm around midday. She tried her best to ignore the mess that had been made of the area as she stepped onto the porch and let herself into the house. After letting a cold Neel out of the refrigerator, she went straight to her bedroom and found the llamas, curled up together on the floor. They stirred as Gretchen curled up with them. Melville raised his head.

"Are you okay?" he asked.

"I will be after some sleep," said Gretchen.

Shelley nuzzled her shoulder, and a few tired hums went up among the others. Neel slid into the room and drifted over to the herd. He gently draped himself over Gretchen's belly without a word.

Epilogue

"You sure you haven't seen the Loch Ness Monster lately?" Gretchen asked Billy for the fourth time in four weeks. She tore off a piece of her sandwich and stuffed it in her mouth.

They sat across from each other at a table by the window at the diner. Penelope and Priscilla occupied the other two chairs. They bent over a stack of legal-looking papers.

Gretchen tilted her head at Billy. She couldn't believe he'd slept through all the action a few weeks ago. The other farmer, whose property backed up to both his and Gretchen's, had high-tailed it out of town the next morning, spewing some sort of nonsense about dragons.

"Nah," said Billy, taking a bite of his own sandwich. "I reckon she was just a stick, like Penelope said." His tone wasn't convincing.

Penelope rolled her eyes and returned to her stack of papers. "Alright, Priscilla," she said, signing the last one. "All the paperwork has gone through, and you are good to go!"

Priscilla smiled and eagerly shook her hand. "Pleasure doing business with you!" She turned to Gretchen. "Thanks for warning me about the copperhead infestation at Elsie's place. I don't know what I would've done if I'd gone through all the trouble of setting up my bed and breakfast only to have the guests get bitten by snakes."

Gretchen nodded. "At least you found a similar property for sale, not too far away!"

"One that isn't infested with snakes," said Priscilla. "Your neighbor seemed pretty eager to move—I can't believe how cheap he was willing to sell the property for. I'm getting it for practically nothing."

Gretchen subtly slipped a piece of ham from her sandwich into her messenger bag and felt a small tug as the bit was wrenched from her fingers.

"We should celebrate!" said Billy. "Miss Snyder has her property, and Gretchen decided to stick around!"

"I have a bottle of champagne, if anyone would like to toast to the success of the bed and breakfast," said Priscilla.

"You had me at 'champagne'," said Penelope.

"I won't say no," said Billy.

The others turned to look at Gretchen.

"I'm invited?" she asked.

"Of course!" said Priscilla.

"Yeah! Absolutely!"

"It's settled, then. You all can come by around six o'clock."

The conversation turned to other matters. At some point, Gretchen's phone buzzed. It was Harley again. She opened the text.

HARLEY
Laser tag this weekend?

Gretchen sighed and typed out a reply.

GRETCHEN
I can't. Got stuff to do.

HARLEY
Come back. I'm bored.

GRETCHEN
Friendship works both ways.

Why don't you come see me?

HARLEY
Okay.

Gretchen stood and stretched. "It was nice having lunch with y'all, and I'm looking forward to tonight, but now I must go feed the llamas. Melville gets cranky if he doesn't get his afternoon snack."

"Do you want a ride home?" asked Billy.

Gretchen shook her head. "I'm fine, thank you."

The others bid Gretchen goodbye as she pulled her messenger bag strap over her head and left the diner.

Sunlight spilled onto the sidewalk, and Gretchen stumbled to the bicycle rack beside the door, blinking out the golden rays as her eyes adjusted.

"Hang in there, Neel. We're about to get on the road."

Neel didn't respond.

"Well, you don't have to take that attitude with me," Gretchen said, undoing her bike lock. She was grateful her mother had remembered to bring it to her. Clambering onto her bike, she set off down the now familiar path through town.

Eventually, she reached a wooded area on the outskirts of town. A dirt path cut through the trees. Gretchen knew it eventually ended up near Elsie's farm—*her* farm—but she hadn't tried it out yet.

"What do you say, Neel?" she said, opening the flap on her messenger bag.

The Eel snaked into the air. He was much larger than he had been a few weeks ago—about as long as she was tall, and as thick as a full-grown python. Somehow, being trapped in the refrigerator had shielded him from the broadcasted shrink ray. The bulb on his head blinked in the shade of the trees as he waited for Gretchen to toss him a piece of jerky from her pocket. She wasn't quite ready to zap him with the shrink ray yet.

Neel didn't answer her question, but shook himself out and drifted toward the woods. Gretchen mounted her bike again.

"I agree."

Test Date: March 15th, Beware!!!
Remember your pencil this time!!!!!

<u>Vocabulary to Know</u>

Amphiuma— A verrrrry loooong salamander with lots of teeth and tiny limbs, perpetually smiling

Artiodactyla— An order of ungulates consisting of species that stand on their fingernails (ouch) and have an even number of toes. Ex: Llamas, giraffes
Side Note: Baby llamas are called "crias" and it's super adorable.

Conspecific— Same species

Herpetology— From the Greek "herpeton", "the study of creeping things", i.e. the study of reptiles and amphibians

Tapetum Lucidum— Tissue layer at the back of the eye that reflects light and makes spooky ghost eyes; llamas are NOT supposed to have them, yet...

Thoracic cavity— Where your heart and lungs are kept prisoners by your rib cage

<u>Dissection Directional Terms</u>

Anterior— Direction pointing towards (toward?) the head of an animal

Posterior— Direction pointing toward (pretty sure there's no "s") the butt of an animal

Dorsal— Direction indicating the backside of an animal

Ventral— Direction indicating the belly side of an animal. Don't pet the ventral side of a cat!

<u>The Life Cycle of Eels</u>

Egg → Leptocephalus (Larva) → Glass Eel → Elver → Yellow Eel → Silver Eel → Adult Eel → Giant Freaking Alien Eel??

ACKNOWLEDGEMENTS

Endless thanks to everyone who has supported me through my first book. I couldn't have done it without you. Special thanks to the Writers of Temple Hall, R. Sapp and A. Gagnon, for being there to bounce ideas off and for encouraging me to actually sit down and finish. Thank you also to A. Harriman, and C. N. Noble, Maeve, Smo, Mom, and Aunt Carla for reading through various stages of my manuscript and for listening as I worked through all the details of this crazy little story.

ABOUT THE AUTHOR

Deep in the city of Memphis, there lives a wild storyteller with her two cats and her snake. Megan Mosier started writing and illustrating odd tales about alien wolves in her fifth-grade classroom, and as time went on, she never stopped. She has continued to hone her skills throughout the years by creating comics and telling stories through RPGs. Her master's degree in biology serves a dual purpose, as she can now accurately describe the biology of her alien wolves in her writing as well as teach college students how to apply the scientific method.

CONNECT

If you liked this story, please consider reviewing it on Amazon or Goodreads.

For updates on new stories, you can sign up for Megan Mosier's newsletter at https://authormeganmosier.eo.page/cpk8n

Thank you so much for reading!

amazon.com/author/meganmosier

goodreads.com/meganmosier

www.ingramcontent.com/pod-product-compliance
Lightning Source LLC
Chambersburg PA
CBHW07085250626
47159CB00003B/1067